bloom

Read more from Simon Pulse

Forever . . .
by Judy Blume

Wild Roses
by Deb Caletti

Lost It
by Kristen Tracy

Sandpiper
by Ellen Wittlinger

Baby Girl
by Lenora Adams

Simon Pulse
New York London Toronto Sydney

This book is a work of fiction. Any references to historical events, real people, or real locales are used fictitiously. Other names, characters, places, and incidents are the product of the author's imagination, and any resemblance to actual events or locales or persons, living or dead, is entirely coincidental.

SIMON PULSE
An imprint of Simon & Schuster
Children's Publishing Division
1230 Avenue of the Americas, New York, NY 10020

Designed by Tom Daly
The text of this book was set in Berkeley.
Manufactured in the United States of America
First Simon Pulse edition April 2007
10
Library of Congress Control Number 2006936715
ISBN-13: 978-1-4169-2683-2
ISBN-10: 1-4169-2683-6

Thanks to Jennifer Klonsky, for taking on this novel and then handling it with so much enthusiasm; Lisa Fyfe, for the gorgeous cover; Robin Rue, for being an amazing agent and always looking out for me; Diana Fox, for her friendship and belief in my work; Anne Greenberg, who helped me see what needed to be fixed; and Micole Sudberg, for her friendship, her thoughts on this book, and for her wisdom at a crucial time.

I'd also like to thank Katharine Beutner, Jessica Brearton, Clara Jaeckel, Amy Pascale, Donna Randa-Gomez, Nephele Tempest, Jane Wilson, and Janel Winter, for reading drafts, for their encouragement, and, most of all, for their friendship. I truly couldn't have done it without you guys!

Thanks also go to my husband, for all his love and support.

Finally, this book is dedicated to Marianna Volokitina,
who always believed I could do this.

one

I guess I kept hoping some kind of miracle would happen. It wasn't even like I was asking for a big one. I mean, I didn't want someone to come along and give me straight A's or perfect hair or anything. I just didn't want to take one lousy class. That's not too much to ask for, right?

A perfectly polished fingernail taps my schedule.

"Told you." Katie and her worry voice. I look up from my schedule—it still has the stupid class listed, damn it—and grin to show I'm okay.

"Lauren," she says, totally not buying it.

I shrug and fold my schedule up real small. I can still see the W in world history, though. I sigh and jam the whole thing in my bag, and then ask, "How many classes do you have with Marcus?"

"None. I thought we might have one, but then . . ." As she keeps talking, I glance over at her. She looks, as always, like she stepped out of a fashion magazine. This is because she gets up at quarter to five every morning. I don't know how she does it. Just thinking about trying to get up that early makes me sleepy.

"Mm," I say, because it's all that's required. A Marcus question guarantees at least five minutes when I don't have to do anything but nod and make vague agreeing noises. Katie's been going out with Marcus for six months now, and he is her entire world. When we first met we used to talk endlessly about how we'd get boyfriends and what we'd do when we had them, and it was only when we actually got boyfriends that I realized without the acquiring of them to talk about, we had absolutely nothing in common.

And that sucks, because Katie's my best friend.

I had a real honest-to-God best friend, Jane, until ninth grade, but then she moved away. At first we talked a lot, like everything was exactly the same even though it wasn't, and then we talked less, and when we did she'd mention people I didn't know and stuff she was doing that I wasn't part of. I'd make up stuff in reply, and before I knew it we weren't talking at all and the only thing I had going on was my volunteer job at the library. You have to do community service in order to graduate, and although most everyone does it at the very last minute, Jane and I had planned it all out before she left. A summer spent among books, but she left and there I was, shelving books and showing people how to use the Internet terminals. Alone.

That's how I met Katie. I'd seen her around but had never really spoken to her—she was more popular than I was; not by a lot but enough so that me saying anything to her was out of the question—but then she started working at the library, and we were shelving books together every day, and one afternoon she just started talking to me. She said she hated the library, and I said I did too, but the truth is I loved it. I love books. I like that the moment you open one and sink into it you can escape from the world, into a story that's way more interesting than yours will ever be. But I could tell Katie wasn't the kind of person you said stuff like that to, so I just asked about her nail polish instead.

After that we talked a lot. She said she was sick of hooking up with guys at parties and wanted a real boyfriend. I hadn't ever hooked up with anyone, much less been to the sort of parties Katie went to, but I wanted a boyfriend too. So we had that in common. Plus it turned out Katie's best friend had decided Katie was a phony and had dumped her in favor of hanging out with the kids who sit around writing awful poetry and calling everyone else shallow. Katie told me that the first time she slept over at my house. I remember she blinked a lot, and I could tell she was trying not to cry, and I knew exactly how she felt. That feeling of being left behind—it sucks. I said those kids were all losers, and Katie grinned at me and asked if I wanted to skip out of work early the next day to go shopping. I didn't really want to; the new books had just come in, and I was going to get to scan them into the system and maybe set aside a couple for myself, but I knew what would happen if I said that. So I said, "Sure, let's go shopping," and we've hung out ever since.

"So what do you think I should do about it?"

I look at Katie, who is biting her lip. "Well," I say hesitantly, because I have no idea what she's talking about, "maybe it's not that big a deal."

"Lauren, he has two classes with Clara. Two. What if she decides she wants him back? What if she—"

"He loves you," I tell her. And it's true. Marcus is totally crazy for her. Katie just worries because before he dated her, Marcus went out with Clara Wright, who is the goddess of Hamilton High and will never ever let anyone forget it. But Marcus and Clara weren't together that long, and besides, Clara is dating some college guy now. Everyone acts like this is a huge deal, but the way I figure it, what kind of college student dates a high school student other than the kind of college student who can't get anyone his own age to actually look at him? Last time I told Katie this she laughed for about ten minutes, but I don't think it would cheer her up this time.

"I know," she says. "I just—not one class! I bet you and Dave have a bunch of classes together, right?"

"I don't know," I say without thinking.

"You don't know? Lauren! You mean you haven't even seen him yet? Why didn't you tell me?" She makes go-away motions, shooing me toward Dave's locker. Toward Dave, who turns to smile at me as if he's heard Katie say my name. For all I know, he probably has. I wouldn't put it past him to have superhearing or something.

You think I'm kidding, but I'm not. Dave is—well, if you saw him you'd understand. He's perfect. And I don't mean that in a he's-my-boyfriend-so-I-have-to-say-that way. He really is perfect. For starters he's a football player, plus he plays baseball. His parents have a whole wall of shelves in their living room filled with trophies he's won. He's got colleges begging him to think about attending even though he's only a junior, and not just for all the sports stuff. His grades are insanely good too.

Also, he's gorgeous: blond hair, blue eyes, tall but not too tall, built but not totally muscle bound. He's so going to be homecoming king when we're seniors. Everyone has a crush on him. Everyone. Until I started dating him, I was a total nobody. But because of him, I'm somebody.

Well, almost. I'm almost somebody, I'm almost popular. And here's the thing about that: It sucks more than being unpopular because I don't fit in anywhere. I thought, when Dave and I first started going out, that people like Clara and those she allows to be her followers would maybe, just maybe, be friends with me. But it didn't work out that way. I could never think of anything to say to Clara that would get her to actually notice me long enough for one of her followers to decide I could be *her* follower, and then Katie started dating Marcus, which Clara took very personally because not only did Marcus not wither away and die after Clara broke up with him, he actually was, you know, happy. So I can sort of hang out with the popular kids if Dave is around, in the sense that I'm in the same place they are, and once in a while one of the girls will ask me where the beer is at a party or something, but that's it. And everyone else—well, they talk about me as if I really am popular. I once walked in on two girls doing that in the bathroom. I could tell because they stopped talking and stared at me.

I said, "Go on, I don't mind," and smiled, and in a movie we would have all become best friends and started braiding one another's hair or something, but instead they just looked at me like I had eight heads. Later I heard them talking about me during lunch. They said I was a bitch and stuff like, "And then she acted like we needed her permission to talk about her!" and so that ended my attempts to be friends with anyone other than Katie.

I was really sad about it for a while. The worst kind of sad too, the kind where you know, deep down, that there's nothing you can do even though you wish you could. I even bought a ton of books with covers that promised stories about girls who seemed to be just like me. I figured maybe there'd be something in them to make me feel better. But they were all about so-called ugly losers who were actually really smart and funny (and quirky cute or even gorgeous to boot) and how the football star or mysterious new boy everyone wants or the best-friend-who-seems-kind-of-ugly-but-actually-really-isn't totally falls in love with them, and they go to the big dance or whatever and learn that it's what's on the inside that counts and crap like that.

I felt a lot worse after reading all those books because I'm not all that smart, and I'm not funny, and I'm not quirky cute or gorgeous. I'm average. Totally average. And worse, I got the football star and look where I am. Still not popular but yet somehow popular enough to be hated, and there was nothing in the books about that, about what to do if your absolute dream came true and yet you stayed you.

That's my problem. I'm . . . well, me. And yet I have a perfect boyfriend. Don't believe me? Okay, take how we started dating. Dave came up to me in the hall right after school started last year and asked me out in front of everyone. Seriously. That's what he did, and I just stood there, staring at him. I finally managed a nod, and I only got that out because Katie kicked me. And then we actually went out, and he did stuff like open my car door and ask if he could kiss me good night, and then e-mailed me when he got home to say he had a great time and when could he see me again? You can't get more perfect than that.

Even his family is perfect. They eat dinner together every night and do stuff like play board games. Board games! Plus his mom and dad are—I swear I'm not kidding—high school sweethearts, and he even has the most adorable little brother in the world, John. For the first two months we went out, I kept waiting for something to happen—for Dave to turn out to be a drug addict, or to actually have like eight other girlfriends, or for him to realize he could do so much better than me—but nothing did. Dave stayed sweet and charming, and at Christmas he gave me a gorgeous locket and told me he loved me as we stood outside while snow was gently falling all around.

See? Perfect. I know I'm totally lucky to have Dave, I do, and if I didn't, the six zillion looks I get when we walk down the halls together would remind me. Take now, for instance. When I get to his locker I can practically hear everyone around us looking and listening as Dave says, "Hey, Lauren," in a soft warm voice and pulls me close, pressing a gentle kiss to my lips.

Totally perfect. Except that, since we've been dating, the farthest we've ever gone happened two months after we started dating. We were at a party and I kept looking at him, wondering what he was doing with me because he could have anyone, and how and when it was all going to end. He noticed I looked worried, of course, and took me to a bedroom to talk. I waited—pretty breathlessly, in all honesty—for him to make a move, but instead he took my hands in his and said he was crazy about me. I said, "Why?" and he said, "Because the first time I noticed you, you were sitting at lunch, looking out a window, and the look on your face—I don't know. I just wanted to hold you." I kissed him then, feeling alive, really alive, for what felt like the first time ever. He kissed me back, and then we were touching, and it was amazing.

And then we stopped. Or rather, he did. One minute he was unhooking my bra and the next he was pushing away from me. He said he was sorry, really sorry, and looked like he was going to throw up. I can't tell you how sexy I felt after that. I remember I buttoned my shirt, my hands shaking, and asked a question I'd been thinking about for a while, the one I was pretty sure I already knew the answer to.

"Are you gay?" I whispered.

I waited for him to say yes. I had this whole thing planned out where he would cry and I would be supportive and people at school would talk, but then they'd totally come around, and Dave and his boyfriend would walk hand in hand down the hall and Clara would be all "Lauren!" when she saw me and invite me to all of her parties, and I'd end up dating this amazingly cute and sensitive artist who'd just come to town but would stay because he'd fallen madly in love with me. But instead of saying yes, Dave said, "What?" like he'd never even heard the word gay before, and then I learned the truth.

Dave's religious. I mean, I already knew that he went to church—it's just about the only thing to do in Hamilton on Sunday—but that's not unusual or anything. But it's more than that for Dave. He looked at me for a second after he'd said, "What?" just staring at me, and then he started talking. He told me that he really wanted to live right, and that it was hard, but he thought it was worth it.

Of all the things I'd thought he'd say, that wasn't one of them. I mean, it's not like anyone at school goes around talking about this stuff, but you could just—you could tell he was happy to talk about it. That he needed to talk about it. So I just sat there, stunned, and listened while he told me about his church and how he'd love it if I would come with him. I listened while he told me that he'd never really talked about what he believed with anyone he'd dated before, but that he was so glad he'd told me, that he knew I was special, that he knew I would understand how important his beliefs were to him.

I listened and nodded, and thought that here I was, in a bedroom with an amazingly hot guy, and what were we doing? Talking about going to church.

If this were one of those novels I'd read that made me feel like crap, Dave would have been gay.

two

Dave walks me to my first class, and we talk about our schedules. No classes together, but we do have the same lunch period. We're holding hands, and he strokes his thumb over mine, says he wishes we had all our classes together. He says he'll be thinking about me all morning and can't wait to see me at lunch. I lean into him a little because his voice sounds so good, and he smells so good, and really, he is gorgeous. He turns and puts a hand on my shoulder, very gently putting some space between us.

"And don't forget you promised to come see John's basketball game on Wednesday night," he says, and kisses me goodbye. I hear the freshman girls that are walking by sigh. Until me, Dave never dated a girl for more than two months. I used to be proud of the fact that people would look at us and wonder why he was still with me. I used to feel as special as Dave always says I am because I knew what mattered most to him. I was the girl he'd chosen to trust.

Now all I can think about is how every time we touch, he's always the first to pull away.

That's the thought that stays with me for most of the day.

My classes are all deadly boring except for music, which flies by because we're playing this great jazz piece that has a clarinet solo. Mr. Herrity lets me play it, and I roar through it, hitting all the notes perfectly. Well, most of them.

"Not bad," he says afterward, and I'm even happier after that because a "not bad" from Mr. Herrity is about the highest praise you can get.

I wash my hands really well after class, but when I meet Katie in the hall she hands me a tin of mints, and then pulls a tube of moisturizer that smells like strawberries from the depths of her purse. I swear, she has everything you could ever want in there.

"You know, it's not too late to have your schedule switched and take trigonometry," she says.

"Oh sure, because the C minus I got in geometry was a sign that I'm meant for advanced math classes."

"We'd get to take it together. We don't have any classes together, just lunch."

I look over at her. She's chewing on her lip and looking down the hallway. "You're going to do fine. You've got a boyfriend who can do all your homework for you."

"Lauren!" she says, but she's smiling. Marcus is a total math genius. He doesn't talk about it much, but he's so good at it that instead of taking math here, he takes some awful-sounding class at the community college. Colleges like Stanford and MIT send him big glossy mailings. The only way I would get something from Stanford or MIT is if I were the last person of almost-college-age left on the planet.

The bell rings and I say, "Don't forget, I'll be done by five, okay?"

She nods. "Just meet me in the parking lot. And have fun with Axel."

I give her the finger, and she laughs and walks down the hall.

When I get to world history the classroom is full, and I look around, hoping to see at least one face I know. No, no—wait. Yes. Over in the far corner is Gail. I'm surprised to see her. Gail's one of those people who always gets A's in everything, but then I remember she was in music with me last year. We've been in music class together for years; before I quit marching band we would sometimes sit together on the bus going to competitions and stuff. I think she plays the flute. I smile at her, and she looks around for a second, like she's checking to see if I'm smiling at someone else or something, and then hesitantly smiles back. I start to cross the room—if I have to suffer through this damn class I might as well sit beside someone I sort of know—but then Axel comes shuffling in.

Axel looks about eighty and has for, I kid you not, at least twenty years. I saw an old yearbook in the guidance office when I was trying to get out of this stupid class, and she looked exactly like she does now, right down to the brown skirt and brown shirt she's wearing. She teaches all the remedial history courses. How she manages to do this, I'll never know.

Actually, I guess I'll find out.

"We'll be sitting in alphabetical order," she barks in a surprisingly loud voice, and points at the last desk in the room. "Young, Shawn. Williams, Cynthia."

And then she just keeps going. At one point Jack Harris, who is repeating his junior year for at least the second time, tries to say something about how the alphabet doesn't start with Z, but she just keeps talking. A couple of people snicker at that, and Jack scowls and starts talking again. Loudly.

This time Axel doesn't keep talking. She just stands there, looking like a strong wind could blow her away, and listens to everything he has to say, most of which can be summed up as follows: "Fuck you."

When he's done, almost everyone laughs, and a couple of people start talking too. Jack looks pretty proud of himself. Then Axel says, "Well, Mr. Harris, thank you for that passionate speech. I'm only sorry it took up so much class time. I was going to give a quiz tomorrow, but now I can't because we're already behind. Therefore, you'll all have to receive F's for your first assignment, which is ten percent of your grade. If you have a problem with this, I suggest you take it up with Mr. Harris. Now, where was I? Oh, yes. Vivnos, Maria."

Jack Harris shuts up after that, probably because of the repeating seniors that are glaring at him. Axel keeps calling out names as though nothing has happened.

I end up sitting in a row of people I don't know (lots of last names starting with S and R, the Os, Ps, and Qs—not so much) because Gail's last name is Adams, which means she's going to be all the way on the other side of the room. Axel is still droning on, finishing up the Ms—when I hear her say, "Kirkland, Evan."

My pen slides across my notebook page, a startled line, and I look at the desk across from mine, at the person who is sliding into it.

Kirkland, Evan.

He's slouched in his seat, feet stretched out in front of him. His hair is dark and longish, falling forward into his eyes, and I can see a long streak of black running up the side of one arm. At first I think it's a tattoo, but then I realize it's dirt or grease or something. There's a patch of it on his jeans too. His hands, resting on the desk, are red, his knuckles scraped, raw-looking, and his fingernails have been bitten down to the quick. And then he looks up, looks at me, and I quickly look away, my stomach knotting.

I haven't seen or thought about Evan Kirkland in years, but suddenly here he is, sitting right across from me.

My dad does real estate development. You know those big subdivisions you drive by, the ones that sell "luxury" homes? He makes them. Hamilton isn't much of a town, but it's near a highway that leads to Broad Falls, which is a huge town and has lots of people who move out here so they can have a really big house. Dad's done most of the subdivisions around here, actually. He designed our house, back when he was first starting out, and one of the few memories I have of my mother is her standing in front of the bay window in the sitting room (really just a fancy name for a room at the front of the house we never use) with her hands pressed against the glass. I remember she jumped when I said, "Mom?" and when she turned around to look at me, it was as if she didn't know who I was. I guess even then she was thinking about leaving.

She didn't; not then, but she did when I was six. Since then it's been me and Dad except for the times he's had a girlfriend and we all got to pretend we're a "family." Dad is not good with women, and all of his girlfriends have moved in and promptly moved right back out. The last one was Robin—she was number four—when I was thirteen. That relationship lasted a year before she left to go back to graduate school (and her old boyfriend). Before her was T'eanna, whose real name was Callie, but she'd just glare at you if you called her that. She was an actress. Dad asked her to move in when I was eleven and a half. She moved in three days after the last girlfriend left, and moved out two days before Robin moved in, although the perfume she wore lingered in the house for about six months afterward. Before her was Sally, whom I hated. She called me "buttercup," which I also hated.

And before her was Mary, whom Dad met the summer I was eight.

I'd been at camp since school let out, and I remember I was so glad to be going home. I'd been afraid something would happen to Dad or that he wouldn't come get me, but he did and even said he had a surprise for me. "Are you ready?" he asked, and when I nodded he said, "We're going to be a family again!"

For a second—one crazy stupid second—I thought he meant Mom had come back. That she'd decided she missed us, that she'd thought about Dad, about me, and wanted to be with us. But then Dad said, "Her name is Mary and, Lauren, you're going to love her," and that was the end of that.

Dad met Mary at a conference the first day I started camp. She was handing out flyers for motivational tapes. He stopped to chat, and two weeks later she moved in. He talked about her all the way home, how she understood him and how much he liked her, and then, right as we were pulling into the driveway, he told me he had another surprise. "She has a son, and he'll be living with us too!" he said, like he'd bought me a pony, and I burst into tears just as the front door opened.

That's when I met Evan.

He and Mary came out of the house hand in hand; Mary smiling big and bright and Evan standing solemn-faced, looking at the car. I was still crying. Dad waved at them and told me, "Come on, sweetheart, don't cry. We're going to be one big happy family!"

I don't think I need to tell you that never happened. The thing about family, that my dad still hasn't learned, is that you can't force it. He's tried five times, and every time it's been a disaster.

Dad and Mary's relationship was good for about three months. Mary cut back on her hours with the motivational tape company so she could "be around for everyone." We did all kinds of stuff together; trips to the park, to the mall, even grocery shopping, and at first the little fights she and Dad had were just laughed off. Then they started saying in too-cheerful voices, "Well, we'll talk about it later." Talking about it later eventually ended in screaming matches punctuated by icy silences that lasted for days.

Evan and I avoided each other the first few weeks, only making mumbled conversation when forced to during dinner. But then one night Dad said, "Lauren, honey, will you pass the rolls to Evan? He didn't eat one," and Evan said, "I said I didn't want any earlier," at the same time I said, "He already said he didn't want any," and after that we got along.

By the time things with Dad and Mary got really bad, I knew that Evan's favorite book was the same as mine, *The Lion, the Witch, and the Wardrobe*, that he hated cola but loved cherry cola, and that his father had died in a car accident when he was four. He knew I would eat chocolate ice cream for every meal if I could, that I hated bees, and that my mother had left and hadn't called or written or anything. Not even a card on my birthday.

We were friends. I can still remember the way he would look at me while I was talking, as if what I was saying was interesting. Not even Mary did that. Heck, not even Dad did that—and he still doesn't. I remember how Evan cried the time we found a bird's nest in the yard, the mother bird's body on the ground, mangled by a cat, and he tried to save the eggs. They never hatched. And when I wrecked my bike while riding lazy loops around the driveway, listening to Dad and Mary talk tensely through an open window, he helped me inside, got bandages, and took the blame when Mary wanted to know who'd tipped their bike into the shrubs she'd just planted.

We fought too, don't get me wrong. He hogged the computer and accused me of always picking crappy television shows to watch. I teased him about his hair—it was like a girl's, really shiny and really soft—but I secretly wished my own was like it, that dark and that pretty. I never said that, of course. He teased me about my eyes, which are, I admit, a little strange. They're gray; light gray, just like Mom's were. And still are, I guess. But after every fight we had, one of us would always say sorry. Always. Dad and Mary never did that.

In the end, they didn't last very long. After those first three months we limped through Christmas and my birthday and a disastrous Valentine's Day when Mary sat in the kitchen waiting for Dad until two in the morning, snapping when either of us asked what was going on. Evan's birthday was a month away, the day he and Mary left. I remember it was marked on our kitchen calendar. She'd packed up all their stuff in boxes, and Dad hollered that there'd better not be anything missing. Mary's face turned red, and she stared at him like he'd hit her. Evan yelled, "Shut up! Don't talk to my mom that way!" and then ran out of the room, out of the house. I looked out the window and saw him sitting in Mary's car.

I went into the hallway, and all his things were in boxes too: the shoes my dad insisted on buying Evan the week he was trying to impress Mary with how generous he was (and to make up for getting home late every single night), the white shirt he had to wear when we all went to get a "family" picture taken.

The picture was still in the living room, waiting to be framed and hung. The yelling got even louder, and Mary was crying. I went up to my room and got the Narnia books Dad had given me for my birthday, a fancy boxed set that Evan had stared at longingly when I'd opened it. I went downstairs and stuffed it at the bottom of one of Evan's boxes, and then ran back upstairs.

When I looked out the window again, Mary was backing her car down the driveway in a hurry, pausing only to clip the mailbox before she pulled onto the road. Her tires left black marks on the street. They were there for a long time.

In the end she had one thing in common with Mom. She couldn't leave fast enough either.

I haven't seen Evan since that day. I asked Dad about him once, a few months after he and Mary left, and he said, "Who?" and then, "Oh, yes. Evan. He's fine, honey. Perfectly fine." It wasn't news to me that grown-ups could lie, but the fact that Dad could forget someone he claimed was family only a few months earlier made me feel awful. Scared. I didn't ask about Evan again.

I found out what happened, though. Mary moved to Florida—I saw the postmark on a letter she sent Dad that he wouldn't let me read but was dumb enough to throw away without shredding. That letter was how I found out about Sally, who was girlfriend number two and moved in soon after, but that's another story and I can't even remember it because I glance over at Evan again and he's looking at me. He has really dark eyes. He looks like he never smiles. I push my pen across my notebook and try to listen to Axel bark about the Persians.

three

I'm so relieved when class is over that I practically race out of the room and down the hall to jazz band practice, grateful to be distracted from the shock of seeing Evan again and how I felt when I looked at him. In my mind he's always looked the way he did when he was eight, all dark, shining hair and quick smiles for Mary, for me, and sometimes even for my dad. But now—I think of his hands again, his fingernails bitten so far down that it must hurt, and the way he looked like he didn't know what a smile was.

We play through all the songs Mr. Herrity has selected for the spring term, and toward the end he throws in the one we played in class today, saying, "Lauren, do the solo please?" I do, but my hands are clumsy, my mind still distracted, and he just nods at me when I'm done and has us all run through the first song again.

He lets us out fifteen minutes early, probably to soften the blow of making us come in for an extra practice tomorrow, and I take my time putting my clarinet away, carefully swabbing it out and then checking my reeds, making sure I have extras and that the one I'm using now is snapped snugly inside its case. Katie won't be outside yet, so no use rushing when I'm just going to end up sitting around, waiting.

When I'm done I eat a few mints and then go to the bathroom. I wash my hands and stand, staring, as water rushes over them. Evan's hands were red, his knuckles scraped raw, like he'd been in a fight. I turn off the water and carefully dry my hands.

"Lauren?"

I realize someone is saying my name and turn to see Gail looking at me quizzically.

"Are you okay?"

I nod.

"You sure? You look . . . I don't know. A little lost or something."

"I'm fine," I say sharply, more sharply than I mean to, and Gail says, "Okay," her face flushing.

"I'm sorry—" I say, but it's too late and she's already out the door. I sigh and head outside.

No Katie. I check my watch: 5:02. Looking around the parking lot, I don't see her car anywhere. Damn. She hasn't forgotten about me—Katie's really great about stuff like that—but she probably went to pick up her brothers and had to talk to their afterschool program head about something. She has to do stuff like that a lot.

I sit down to wait for her. I wish I had a car but Dad won't let me use his or our other one. He says it's because he doesn't trust other drivers, but I know he means he doesn't trust me. I think deep down he worries that if I have a car I might do what Mom did, that he might come home one day and find me gone. Not that he would ever admit that, even if I pushed him. But I think that's part of it.

The other part might be that before he stopped letting me drive, I got three speeding tickets.

At 5:10 I look around the lot again. Still no Katie. She probably took Marcus with her, and he never locks his car so I can go sit in it and wait.

Except Marcus's car isn't in the lot either. Shit. That means her brothers took the bus home, and Marcus and Katie are at his house. Now I'll have to wait here till 6:30, when Marcus's mom gets home and Katie has to sneak out his window because Marcus's mom already thinks they spend too much time together. I think about calling Dad, but he'll be in a meeting or at a job site and I'll have to leave a message, and by the time he gets it it'll be after 8:00. Plus I'm not even sure if he knows where the high school is.

I think about doing homework, but decide against it. It's bad enough I have to sit around waiting for Katie, who will no doubt drive me home with a huge grin on her face and tell me all about the great sex she and Marcus just had. I'll have to nod and act like it's exactly the same for me because the one time

Katie asked about me and Dave, I couldn't bring myself to say that we weren't doing what everyone assumed we were. To be honest, I can't even picture Dave and me having sex. Although . . . I close my eyes, think about Dave's hands on my body, cupping my ankles, sliding up across my legs, circling over my knees. I think about how I would look down and see his hands, feel the roughness of his split knuckles when he turned his fingers to trace—wait. Dave doesn't have split knuckles. Damn. I feel my face flame bright red and, lucky me, just in time for Mr. Herrity to come out and say, "Lauren, are you feeling all right?"

"Fine," I mumble, and don't let myself press a hand to my stomach, which is knotted and jumping.

"Someone coming to pick you up?"

I nod.

"Good," he says, and adds, "Make sure you practice that piece we played in class today," before he strides off into the parking lot.

What does that mean? That he thinks I suck? But if he thought that, why would we be playing the piece again? I worry about it for a few minutes and then look at my watch again: 5:18.

I sigh and open my backpack. I have a bunch of assignments already. During fall term, teachers usually go easy on the homework for the first few days. But in spring, forget it. I even have homework in Axel's class. You'd think her endless lecture would have been enough, but oh no, we have reading to do, and she'll probably talk about it tomorrow and I'll be stuck sitting there with Evan Kirkland across from me.

Evan again? What is wrong with me? I dig through my bag

until I find the book I'm reading and drag it out. No one is around, so I don't have to worry about anyone seeing me. I can't wait till college, honestly. I don't know where I'm going yet—my only criteria is that it's somewhere far away—but when I get there I'm going to major in English and spend four (well, knowing me, it'll probably be more like five or six) years reading books.

I read until I hear a bunch of people come out, loud voices laughing and saying really lurid things about Clara Wright. I shove my book back into my bag and listen. After a particularly detailed story that ends with Clara screaming, "Jack Harris is a GOD!" I realize I'm listening to the detention kids, who Clara wouldn't even look at, much less have sex with. I watch them head into the parking lot and fan out toward their cars. A few more people trickle out, and I notice a couple of them looking over in my direction. I brace myself for a conversation that will consist of them speculating on what keeps Dave interested (if they only knew it was my ability to attend church on Sundays and keep my clothes on), but they just head out into the parking lot.

I look at my watch again: 5:23. Sigh. I'm hungry, I'm tired, and I want to go home. I could get my book out again or, better yet, call Katie and find out where the hell she is.

As I'm digging around in my bag for my phone and hoping I remembered to actually charge it, I realize that a car is stopped at the end of the sidewalk and that the person inside is looking at me. I hear the whir of a passenger window rolling down. Evan.

His hair looks very dark in the fading light, and his eyes, watching me, seem to be somehow even darker. He isn't smiling.

"Do you want a ride?" he says. His voice is very quiet. He

doesn't sound at all like I remember. Mary called him "chatterbox" sometimes because she said he talked so much.

"I—" I say, and look around, unsure. If there's a way to deal with seeing someone who makes you feel kind of dizzy and strange when you look at him, I sure don't know it.

"Never mind," he says, voice sharp and weary at the same time, and the passenger window starts to roll back up, his face disappearing.

"Wait," I say, and stand up. I walk down the sidewalk. When I finally get to his car, I don't know what to do with my bag or my clarinet case, and end up sort of stumbling/falling into the seat. I feel my face flame red as my head knocks against Evan's shoulder.

"Sorry," I mutter, and arrange myself as best I can, clarinet case by my feet and bag on my lap, like it's some sort of cover. He starts the car and I'm very glad, afraid that the rapid thud-thudding of my heart was audible before.

He doesn't say anything. Not as we're leaving school, not when we're pulling onto the main road. I look over at him when we're stopped at the traffic light that feeds onto the road that just about all the subdivisions are on, and he's looking at me. Our eyes meet for a second, and he looks away quickly. I feel strange, totally unable to focus on anything except the fact that we're sitting very close.

"Um, I live—" I say, my voice coming out shaky, hesitant.

"Same place as . . . as before?" he says.

All I can manage is a nod. I feel like I did the one time I almost fainted. There was a moment, right before my vision tunneled and I was told to sit down, when everything seemed to be too bright and strong, as if I was seeing something hidden in what had always been, as if what I knew as real was just a shadow of what really was.

I don't remember the rest of the drive, not really. I remember thinking I should say something, but instead I saw his hands on the steering wheel and stared at them, at his knuckles. I remember feeling my breath catch when I thought about the daydream I'd had about Dave and how it wasn't about Dave at all.

I remember that when he saw me looking, he folded his fingers in, hiding his fingernails from my sight. I remember his left leg tapped when we were stopped at a four-way stop, jittering out a restless rhythm. I remember when we pulled onto my road he let out a sharp breath, like someone had hit him, and said, so softly I don't think I was meant to hear him, "It looks the same."

I remember he stopped at the end of my driveway, and I sat there for a second before realizing he wasn't going to go any farther, that he wasn't going to drive up to the house. I remember I turned back once I'd gotten out of the car, fumbling with my bag and my clarinet case. He was watching me again, and this time when our eyes met, he didn't look away.

I meant to say, "Thank you," politely, maybe even regally, as if the whole thing had been no big deal, but what came out was his name.

"Evan," I said, and we both twitched a little at that, like there was a live current running between us.

"I gotta go," he said, and leaned over and pulled the door closed. I didn't look back to see him leave, but I heard him, the roar of his car fading as he vanished down the road.

four

I'm the first person home, of course. I'm always the first person home. I check my voice mail and my e-mail, then try to decide if I could somehow purchase a car online and have Dad not find out about it. I bet he wouldn't notice it. At least not until the credit card bill came. That he notices. ("Lauren, did you really need to spend eighty-five dollars for a haircut?") His problem is that he has no idea how much things cost. I can't wait till we have to talk about college tuition.

I work on homework for a while, though my history book stays wedged firmly at the bottom of my bag. I get a glimpse of it once, just once, and it's like I'm back in the car with Evan again. Evan. I look down and see I've typed his name into the essay I'm supposed to be writing for English. I hit the backspace key and the four letters disappear. After I end up typing his name another three times, I give up on the homework and go downstairs.

Tonight's dinner is some meal-in-a-bag thing I got the last time I went to the grocery store. Dad would rather spend his free time working, so the minute I got my license it became my job to make sure we have food, which is fine with me as going to the store is pretty much the only time he actually allows me to drive anywhere. As for cooking, I'm definitely the only one who does that. Robin, the last girlfriend, was a pretty good cook, and for a while there were fancy dinners every night. Then Dad started coming home late or missing dinner altogether, and the meals stopped.

I picked up a few things though, and for a while after she left I was making myself stir-fries and stuff. But the thing about cooking is that you have to clean up afterward, so it's easier just to make something that comes in its own container or uses one pan. I eat at the kitchen table, staring out at the pool in the backyard.

Dad had it put in for Sally, who'd grown up near the ocean and said she missed it, and when we first got it Jane and I made all these huge plans about how I would invite people over to swim and then suddenly everyone would want to hang out at my house, with us. But when I finally worked up the nerve to ask—you guessed it—Clara, she said, "I go to the club pool," and that was that. She meant the country club down the road, the one all the families with parents who commute to Broad Falls belong to. I hear they have eight pools or something. I used to nag my dad to join when I was younger, but what's the point? If Dave can't make me popular, joining the country club sure won't.

Now our pool sits pretty much unused, although once a year Dad will decide he wants to get more exercise and swims laps every morning for a week or two. Katie and I sort of use it in the summer, working on our tans and checking out the cleaning guy if he's cute. He usually isn't. Cute pool boys are another only-in-books thing. Either that or they all work at the country club.

When I'm done with dinner, I practice the piece Herrity made us play in class and then do laundry and more homework. Dad sends all his stuff—and I mean all of it, even underwear—to the cleaners, but I just don't like the idea of someone washing out my socks. Or my underwear. And plus they put starch all over everything, and jeans that have been starched? There's no end to the discomfort. Also, I like the sound the washer and dryer make. Without them the house would be so silent that I'd probably be able to hear myself breathing. I find myself thinking about Evan again as I'm folding my shirts, about the mark on his arm, about his hands, his eyes, his hair. About him looking at me.

"Quit it," I tell myself, and put my clothes away.

Dad comes home when I'm downstairs watching television. It takes him about eight hundred minutes to come inside because he has to cover his car so it doesn't get scratched (apparently parking in the garage isn't enough to protect it) and then, while he's doing that, he always checks his voice mail and ends up returning all his messages. When I was younger I used to go out to the garage and listen to him talk, but you can only hear so many conversations about windows and "open space" and the many shades of beige before you get bored. Plus Dad is still in work mode when he's on the phone, and the most acknowledgment I could ever get from him was a quick wave and the just-a-second finger gesture which I soon learned meant, "Not until I'm done with all these calls."

Katie and I were talking about college once, and she said she hated the idea of having a roommate. "I just want my own space, you know?" she said, and I said, "Totally," but the truth is I'm kind of looking forward to it. I have so much space that I wouldn't mind giving a little bit of it up.

When Dad finally comes in, I hear him drop his briefcase on the kitchen counter and sort through the mail. "Lee Lee?" he says. "You down here?"

I turn the television up louder. Some people like nicknames. I am not one of them. This is because every time I hear mine I'm reminded of how awful my name really is. Lauren Smith is boring but my full name is—well, okay. My full name is Lauren Lee Smith. Of all the names I could have been given, that's the one I got. Lauren Lee Smith. It has all the personality of a toaster. It could be a toaster. The Lauren Lee Smith model.

Dad comes into the living room and turns the television off. "Lauren."

"Hi!" I say brightly. He sighs and then grins at me.

"You're a stubborn one, kiddo." See? With the nicknames? Awful.

"Look who's talking."

"Ah, but you're stubborn in a different way," he says. "You're like—" He breaks off, and I can tell he's tired because the only time he slips up and almost mentions Mom is when he's not sleeping well, and that never happens unless things at work aren't going perfectly.

"Come sit down," I tell him. "I'll make you something to eat."

He settles down on the sofa and I head into the kitchen. He's asleep by the time I get back. I leave the sandwich I made on a plate on top of the piano, which, by the way, has never really been played. It was T'eanna/Callie's idea for me to learn, so I could help her practice for musical roles. I got through about four lessons before she decided she wanted to focus on film work.

As I'm going upstairs my dad says, "Hey, Lauren?"

"Yeah?"

"How was your day?"

I saw Evan today, I think about saying. *Remember him, Dad?* But instead I say, "Fine." And when Dave and I talk later, a quick instant message session as I'm trying to finish my homework, that's what I say too. That I'm fine. Perfectly fine.

When I'm brushing my teeth before I go to bed, I look at myself in the mirror. Straight brownish hair, my mom's gray eyes. I have her nose too, right down to the freckles scattered across it. Sometimes I wonder if the reason why Dad doesn't spend all that much time at home is because a reminder of her lives there. I flip off my bathroom light and crawl into bed, stare up at my ceiling. It takes me a long time to fall asleep.

* * *

Katie comes inside to pick me up in the morning, apologizes eight hundred million times for yesterday and for not calling last night, and then says, "So how did you get home?"

"I—is that ink on your shirt?" I ask.

"What? Oh crap! I thought I got it out. I was trying to finish my stupid English homework this morning, and so I'm sitting there, writing, and all of sudden there's a lizard in my lap. A lizard! I've told Harold and Gerald it's not funny when they do that but . . . " She sighs. "Kids."

"You sound like you're thirty or something," I say, and pass her a wet paper towel, very happy she's forgotten her question about how I got home.

She flushes a little and dabs at her shirt. "I'm just tired," she mumbles. "They both want to have a huge birthday party 'cause they're turning nine, and I don't know how I'll make the arrangements and keep up with all the housework, and then there's school and—" She breaks off. "There. I think I got it. Can you see the spot?"

I shake my head. Katie doesn't talk about home stuff very often, and when she does she always sounds like this. I don't get it. I mean, Harold and Gerald have awful names—they're already twins, so isn't giving them rhyming names just too cruel?—but they aren't bad kids. In fact, they actually listen to Katie when she tells them to do stuff. The one time I tried babysitting, I couldn't even get a three-year-old to listen to me.

"You know what you should do? Tell your mom to have

it at that laser tag place. Dave's brother had his last birthday party there."

"I'll do that," she says, and throws the paper towels away, then puts my breakfast plate in the dishwasher. She's such a neat freak. "You ready to go?"

When we get to school, Katie parks in her usual spot and "bumps into" Marcus. We walk in to school together, or rather they walk ahead of me, arms suction-cupped around each other with one of Marcus's hands occasionally sliding down to touch her ass. Dave comes up to me as we're passing through the cafeteria to the wing where all the junior lockers are and greets me with a kiss on the forehead, wrapping his arms around me for a quick hug.

"Let me get that," he says, and takes my backpack, hefting it onto his shoulder so it rests on top of his bag.

"Thanks," I say, and look over at him. I swear, even his teeth are perfect. And he never even had braces!

"John's really glad you're coming to his game," he says. "We were practicing last night, and I think he might get to go to the state skills challenge this year. Wouldn't that be great?"

Is that Evan walking down the hall? I think it's him, way at the far end. Walking toward us.

"Absolutely," I say, and Dave squeezes my hand. We stop at Marcus's locker, and he and Dave fall into a conversation about some sports thing. Katie rolls her eyes at me and then checks her shirt again.

"It's fine," I tell her, and look away just in time to see Evan less than five feet away from me. There's no mark on his arm today. One of his sneakers has a hole at the toe, a little ragged tear. He shoves his hair out of his face with one hand. Even under the awful greenish florescent lights it glows darkly. He's taller than Dave, I realize. When I kiss Dave I just have to tilt my head up a little. To kiss Evan I'd have to look up. I'd have to reach up. I'd put my hands on his shoulders, and when he bent down toward me, his hair would brush my face. I'd close my eyes and—

"Who are you looking at?" Katie nudges me in my side. Evan is walking right by us. He is looking at me. I wonder if he can tell what I'm thinking. I feel like it must be written all over me.

"Nothing," I say too loudly, too brightly, and lean over to rest my head against Dave's shoulder. He leans back and kisses the top of my head. A chorus of little sighs from freshmen walking by, and out of the corner of one eye I see Evan still walking down the hall, and I watch him fade into the crowd of people heading to class.

I try not to think about world history at the end of the day, and so naturally by lunch it's all I can think about. Clara favors Dave with a smile on her way to her seat—she sits at the far end, but the whole table is hers and everyone knows it. Katie and I are sort of allotted seats, in the sense that every day we walk up with Dave and Marcus, and every day we're given a variety of do-I-know-you? looks. Clara tells Marcus "Hi," and then stops, leans down, and whispers something in his ear, watching Katie the whole time. Katie pretends not to notice, but I see her put down the piece of pizza she was picking at, her mouth a tense line.

I lean over and whisper, "He's not even listening." And he really doesn't seem to be. He's nodding the way all guys do when girls are talking about something they aren't interested in—which means anything other than sex, music, or sports. (Except for Dave. He always listens.)

Katie doesn't say anything, but I hear her exhale in relief when Clara saunters off.

"What did she want?" the guy next to Marcus asks, awe in his voice. I wish I could kick him.

"Just telling me about some party this weekend," he says, and then asks Dave, "You going?"

"Nah. Got other stuff to do."

There's some knowing laughter and the usual guy crap, where they all look at him and say stuff about us. Dave grins, looking totally unconcerned, but then, as it continues and gets a little more graphic, his ears turn red. Eventually he pushes away from the table and stands up.

"You want to go for a walk?" he says, and I nod.

"Sorry," he says when we're outside, and I think about how everyone probably figures he stepped in to save me from being embarrassed and how that isn't the case at all.

"So you're doing something this weekend?" I ask.

"My parents want to go to this family retreat thing. We've been talking about visiting schools, but this will be a chance for us to really make plans and stuff. Do you want to come?"

No way. I went on one family retreat. We spent the whole weekend in the woods, talking about our feelings and making plans for our future. Dave and I had been dating about four months at that point, and I thought that bit was kind of cool. I mean, not only did I have a boyfriend, I had a boyfriend who was happy to talk about our future. But since then, all Dave and I have done is talk, so I'm not feeling a need to go away to do that. Plus I like staying in places with running water. And toilets.

"I think I'd better stay here. I told Katie a while ago that I'd go to some party with her and Marcus. You know she's worried Clara will decide she wants him back."

Dave nods. "Next time, then," he says, and I'm saved from replying by the bell and more classes. I pretend to listen through them when in reality I'm thinking about history. By the time I walk into the classroom it's like everything inside me is—I don't know. Turned up too loud or something. I feel on edge, strange, and then I notice the desk across from mine is empty.

I sit down, stare at my desk. I feel deflated now, let down. Why? I think I know. Then Evan walks into the room, and I know for sure because the moment he does, the feeling of before comes back even stronger. He sits down and I can see one of his sneakers, the one with the tear at the toe. If I follow my gaze up a little I can see his knee. A little more and I can see—I look back at my desk. I'm very definitely feeling on edge now.

Axel comes clomping into the room and starts talking. Jack Harris, who I guess has rallied from yesterday, says something loudly a few minutes after she's started. Axel stops talking and claps her hands together slowly, sarcastically, and then asks if he'd like to continue and make us all flunk another quiz. Then she starts right where she left off. No one says anything else.

I want to look at Evan so bad it kind of scares me. I manage to make it about halfway through class before I crack. He's leaning forward a little, writing in his notebook. His hands—I don't even know the word to use for them. They're still rough looking, his nails still bitten down raw, but his fingers are long, and I watch them flex as his hand moves gracefully across the page. Axel makes a point about something by screeching chalk across the board, and Evan looks up. I'm staring, I know I am, but I can't help myself. His hands still. He looks over at me. He smiles a little, a tiny chewed-off smile.

I smile back. He blinks as though I've startled him and looks down. Then he looks at me again. I feel like everything around me is gone, the whole world reduced to us and how we are looking at each other. It's like the fact that we used to know each other is there, and matters, but there's something else. Something more.

I think about that and how I have jazz band practice again today. How I'm going to have to wait for Katie afterward.

And how I hope I'll see him.

five

I do see him.

After jazz band practice I find myself, as predicted, waiting for Katie. This time, however, I'm not all that anxious for her to show up, and when a car that looks like hers pulls into the parking lot, I feel my heart sink. It isn't her, and I let out a shaky breath, pull out my cell, and call her. It goes straight to her voice mail (she must still be with Marcus), and I tell her I have a ride home. Then I hang up and feel really stupid. I fiddle with my bag, call her voice mail again, and then hang up because the detention kids are leaving, slouching their way to their cars. As the last of them trickle out I see Evan. He looks over at me for a second and then looks away. I'm dimly aware of the parking lot clearing out. Mostly I'm aware that I'm standing here like a frozen lump. That I'm waiting. Hoping.

When the last of the detention kids drive off, Evan looks over at me again. And then he's walking toward me. I start to shove my book in my bag, and then think maybe that will look strange, like I was just waiting for him to show up or something. I end up with my hand wedged in my bag like it's gotten stuck there or something. It's funny, but I've never felt quite so flustered or stupid around Dave. Ever.

Evan stops a few feet away from me and shoves his hands in his pockets.

"Do you need a ride?"

I nod, and we walk in silence to his car. I know I should say something, anything, but the truth is that if you asked me to spell my name right now, I'm not sure I could. I keep sneaking looks at him out of the corner of one eye, staring at the way his hair falls across the nape of his neck, the way the hem of his shirt is a little frayed. When we get to the car he unlocks my door first, and then stands there for a second, back to me. Then he opens the door—it squeaks madly—and turns to face me. His face is a little flushed.

"Just throw the stuff on the seat in the back," he mutters.

I gather up a couple of shirts, a pair of jeans, and one of those huge plastic soda cups they sell at gas stations, then push it all into the back. He seems to keep all his clothes in the car. I didn't notice that yesterday. But then I didn't notice much of anything besides him.

We leave the school in silence too. I pick at my bag and feel stupid. I wish I could say something, but I can't. It's like I'm paralyzed by how badly I want to talk to him. By how I can't think of the right thing to say. But I should say something. Anything. Two words. One, even.

At the traffic light his hands flex on the steering wheel.

"How—" he says quietly. "How was band practice?"

"I'm not . . . I'm not in band."

He looks at me and a smile blooms across his face. A real honest-to-God smile. I feel like I can't breathe.

"You sure?" he says, and he's still smiling and looking at me. At my clarinet case. Oh hell.

"I'm in jazz band."

"Ah," he says, and his voice is still quiet but not nearly as serious, almost playful. "Big difference, I guess. What do you play?"

I have not voluntarily discussed music with anyone in years. Dad doesn't know, I don't think—he's never home when I practice, and I've never bothered inviting him to any of my concerts. Katie and I refer to it only indirectly, in the way she's always passing me mints or moisturizer. Dave asked about it when we were first going out, and even mentioned wanting to see/hear me play, but I always changed the subject, reluctant to talk about it, and eventually he stopped asking. But now I hear myself saying, "Clarinet. For about seven years."

"You any good?"

"No."

He laughs, and if I had trouble not staring at him before, now it's even worse. When he laughs his whole face lights up, and when he looks over at me again his grin is relaxed, sunny, and his eyes are sparkling.

For the rest of the ride we talk about music. He asks about the songs we're playing, and before I know it I'm telling him about the one with the solo, the one we played in class and that Mr. Herrity has been having us go over during practice too.

"I keep hoping he'll pick it for the concert but—"

"So I might get to hear you play during an assembly or something?"

"No way," I say, and his smile fades. "I mean, we don't play at school. And if we did, I'd have to quit because I don't want anyone to know that I'm in jazz band." I'm aware of what an incredibly stupid thing I've said as soon as I've finished saying it. "I mean, not that you're—"

"I get it," he says, and his mouth has compressed into a thin tense line.

"No, it's just—I wasn't thinking," I say. "I mean, I don't talk about music much. My dad doesn't even know I still play. It's . . . private, or something. Something that's just mine."

I dare a glance over at him. He still isn't smiling, but he's looking at me and the way he is makes my breath catch. He's looking at me like I'm the only thing he sees. A car behind us beeps its horn, and we both start a little.

"I get it," he says again, but now it sounds totally different.

We talk a little more about music. He says he was in a band for a while. "Not a very good band," he says with a grin, "but it was fun while it lasted."

"What instrument did you play?"

"The triangle."

I laugh. "The triangle?"

"It was an experimental band."

"Uh huh. Let me guess . . ." I look at him and tilt my head a little to one side, studying him. "You played keyboards."

He grins. "What gave it away?"

"The fact that at Christmas you wouldn't stop playing that awful keyboard you got. I still can't listen to anyone play 'Chopsticks.'"

"Oh, you know you were just jealous of my natural talent."

"Yeah, it takes a genius to butcher a song with what, four notes in it?"

"I really loved that thing," he said. "But Mom threw it away after we left. She said it reminded her of—" He falls silent. We both do. We both know how the sentence was going to end. My dad bought the keyboard for Evan, and it reminded Mary of him.

"So what happened to the band?"

"Split up."

"Why?"

"Because I moved here," he says.

"Oh," I say. "I'm sorry." I want to ask where he's been, about the long-ago letter Mary sent from Florida and how Evan ended up there and then back here, but I can tell mentioning anything remotely related to Dad isn't a good idea.

He shrugs. "It's just as well. With work and everything I didn't have much time for it."

"Well, maybe you could start another one or something," I say. "I mean, you won't be in detention forever, right?"

"Detention?"

"Yeah, the whole stay-after-school thing, you know?" I grin at him.

"I'm not—I stay after school to do homework. If I went home, by the time I got there I'd only have about an hour before I have to leave for work so it's just easier to—" He breaks off. We've turned onto my road.

"Oh." I don't want our conversation to end like this. I don't want it to end. "Where—" I clear my throat. "Where do you work?" I try to think what store at the mall he might work at. I know—well, okay, I occasionally get told hello by—two girls who work at the one high-end boutique, and Katie worked at the pizza place last summer. Neither of those places seem like somewhere he'd work.

"Anderson Freight."

"The—the warehouse?" No one I know works at the warehouse. It's this huge—well, warehouse, and one of the few actual businesses left in Hamilton, which was a factory town until they all shut down and the Broad Falls workers started moving in. Anderson supposedly ships stuff—lumber or something—all over the country. I know some people's parents work there, but someone my age? Never. "I didn't know they hired part-time."

"They don't."

I stare at him. "Then how do you work there?"

He smiles at me, but it's not really a smile. It's a mocking upward curve, a smile that isn't, and I can't tell if it's directed at me or him or both of us. "I work nights when I can. It's not exactly an official job, but they pay really well if you can work six to two."

"That's awful," I say, and he flinches as though I've hit him.

"I have to," he says fiercely. "I need a job."

"Why?"

He just looks at me. I feel very stupid suddenly. Why does anyone need a job? Money. "Sorry. What—what do you do?"

"Freight," he says shortly.

"Freight?"

"Unloading trucks," he says. "Look, I shouldn't have said anything. I . . . Promise me you won't tell anyone. They pay me under the table so they don't have to use union guys, and if anyone found out—I can't afford for that to happen."

I can't believe he works at Anderson. And what he does—I guess that explains the grease mark on him the first day I saw him. I look at him now, and he's sitting looking straight ahead, hands tight on the steering wheel like he's angry. I open my door, gather my stuff together. I look back, and he's still sitting exactly the same except now I see he isn't angry. He looks tired. Alone. There's a bruise on his right hand. I lean over and touch the skin below it, right along the line of his wrist. The second I do I know it's exactly what I've wanted to do since I first saw him again. I wanted to touch him. I want to touch him.

"I won't tell anyone," I say, and he turns and looks at me, his hand moving, his fingers sliding along my own.

And now I know what else I want. I want him to touch me.

six

The next morning I tell Katie she doesn't need to give me a ride home after school.

"How come?" she says, motioning for me to pick up the piece of granola bar wrapper I accidentally dropped on the car floor.

"Neat freak," I say as I do, teasing her. And changing the subject. "I don't know how you manage to keep this thing so clean. What do you do with your brothers? Bribe them not to drop anything?"

"Yep," she says, and grins at me. "Are you sure you don't want me to wait for you? I don't have to pick Harold and Gerald up till after four, so I don't mind."

"It's okay, I'm just going to the library," I say casually. Well,

I try to. Actually it comes out way too rushed and more like, "It'sokayI'mjustgoingtothelibrary."

"You can't walk there! Well, you could, but they'd be closed by the time you got there."

"No," I say. "The school library."

"The school library?" What's not said, but what I hear perfectly well, is "The place where total losers hang out and even then only during lunch so no one will have to see that they can't find someone to sit with?"

"Yeah. See . . ." Think, Lauren, think! Why on earth would I have to go to the school library?

Evan. But I can't say that. But I can say—

"Axel," I say, and then, more confidently, "Axel. She wants us to write an essay."

"And only use the school library?"

I nod and mentally cross all my fingers and toes.

"Figures. Everyone in her classes is so stupid she probably figures they couldn't find the actual library."

I clear my throat. When she looks over at me, I raise an eyebrow and mock glare.

"Not you, dumbass," she says with a grin. "Even if you do eat chocolate-covered marshmallow bars for breakfast."

"Chocolate-covered marshmallow *granola* bars. Granola's nutritious."

"You sound like Harold and Gerald."

"You sound like a mom." I wonder if mine would sound like that if she were still around. Somehow I doubt it.

I wait for Katie to laugh, but she just sighs and says, "Yeah."

"You okay?" I ask.

"Just tired," she says, and we pull into the school parking lot. "Let me know if you change your mind about a ride home."

I nod and look out the window. When I came up with this plan last night, it seemed like a really good one. But now I can see Dave walking toward us. The sun is glinting off his hair, and everyone's head turns to follow him as he walks across the lot. He looks almost too perfect to be real, and he's smiling at me.

"Hey," he says when I get out of the car, and for a second it is just like something out of a movie: me—the ordinary girl—getting out of the car, and him—the perfect guy—taking my hand and smiling at me. Except that's how it feels. Like I'm watching a movie. Looking at his hand holding mine, I don't feel much of anything except worry that I don't feel more of anything. When we first started going out I felt so much—amazement that he wanted to date me, nervousness because I kept wondering when he'd decide he didn't want to anymore. Now I know exactly what he's going to say, and "6:30" is out before he's finished saying, "What time should I pick you up tonight?"

"You two might as well be married," Marcus says, coming up behind us and wrapping his arms around Katie. She laughs like it's the funniest thing ever and they walk toward school, suctioned-cupped against each other again.

I roll my eyes at Dave. He smiles down at me and says, "I guess we're just the perfect couple."

There's no such thing, I want to say. But I don't because if

I did, Dave would argue that of course there could be, just look at his parents. Just look at us.

"I guess so," I tell him, and we walk into school holding hands, stopping every couple of feet because someone wants to talk to him. As we reach the hallway where our lockers are, we pass Evan. He's leaning against a wall, nodding at something someone's saying to him. I can't really see who he's talking to—too many people walking by—but I can see Evan. He doesn't look like he's from a movie. The bruise on his hand has turned a yellowish green, and he's got a scrape on his jaw, a thin red line, angry-looking under the lights. He looks tired. He looks real.

"I know I promised last week I'd drive you home today," Dave is saying. "But—well, I promised I'd go talk to Coach about my training schedule. He thinks we have a good chance of getting to the state finals, and I really don't want to let him down."

Evan looks away from whomever he's talking to, and our eyes meet for a second. Just a second, but it's enough for me to feel a million different things.

"It's okay," I say. "I don't mind."

After school I go to the library. I've never been, but it's exactly the way I thought it would be, deathly quiet and row after row of books that look like they've never been touched. The librarian looks surprised when I walk in, and then narrows her eyes as I walk down the aisles, as though she thinks I might suddenly start stuffing books in my bag or something. I suppose actually seeing someone in here is probably a shock, but still. I trail my hand along one shelf just to mess with her—I can see why no one ever comes here; I mean, does any library need ten copies of *Moby-Dick*?—and then smack my fingers into the end of it because I see Evan sitting at a table, looking at me.

I don't know what's worse, the fact that my hand cracking into the shelf makes the loudest sound ever or the fact that it hurts so bad I think I may have broken all my fingers. The librarian clears her throat, and when I look over at her, she points at a sign that says QUIET, PLEASE.

"There go my plans to lie on the floor and start screaming," I mutter, and I guess it's even quieter in there than I thought because I watch her mouth quirk, briefly, before her eyebrows draw together. I hear not-very-well-muffled laughter and look over, see Evan grinning at me. The librarian clears her throat again, and he turns his laugh into a cough.

I smile at him and he smiles back for a second, a wide real grin so gorgeous it's almost lethal, then looks down at his book. Then he glances back up at me.

And okay, this was as far as my go-to-the-library-and-see-Evan plan went. And to be honest, it didn't include me smacking my hand into a shelf, although I have to admit I'm not minding all that much since Evan is still smiling at me. But I have no idea what to do now. Clearly I need to work on my planning skills.

I turn back around and look at the shelf. I don't think any of these copies of *Moby-Dick* have ever been checked out. I fiddle with one of them while I try to think of what to do next.

"Hey." Evan. He's standing right next to me, close enough so that when I look over at him our elbows brush. "Is your hand all right?"

Just once can't I be the kind of girl who can walk into a room and toss her hair just so? Must I always be—well, me? I look at my hand, wiggle my fingers. They all work. The only thing I've hurt is my dignity. Figures. "Yeah."

"You sure?" And then he reaches over and takes my hand, holding it in his while he looks down at my fingers. Forget the hair tossing. This was the greatest idea ever. I should think of something to say. Quickly.

"What are you doing here?" Oh, excellent question. Never mind that he already told you he comes here to do homework, Lauren. Now he can think you're clumsy *and* stupid. Wonderful.

"Studying," he says. "You?"

"Um—just. You know. Studying. Also." Great. Very brilliant. I pull my hand away from his and look back at the shelf. Perhaps it could just fall on me now and put me out of my misery. I can see it now. Lauren Smith, dead from embarrassment and an avalanche of Melville. It'll look super on my tombstone.

He's silent for a second, and I dare another look at him. He's looking at me, but the second I look at him he glances at the shelf, shoves his hands into his pockets. "Do you—do you maybe want to come sit with me?"

I stare at him. It's not that I don't want to. Obviously I do, since I'm here in the school library, for heaven's sake. But to just come right out and ask? I wish I'd thought of that.

He's looking back at me, and he's not smiling. In fact, he's almost scowling at me. I suddenly realize that he's nervous, just like me, but he went ahead and took a chance. People don't usually do that. I mean, I know people think teenagers hang naked out of cars and whatever, but you know, high school really isn't an environment that encourages you to do anything other than exactly what everyone else is doing. It never occurred to me that things could be, you know, easy. But they can be because when I say, "Sure," it comes without any problem at all.

The librarian gets up and makes a circuit around the room when I sit down across from Evan, pausing in front of the shelf I banged my hand into and carefully checking every book, counting the row of *Moby-Dick* copies three times before heading back to her desk. "I guess I should have stuffed some of them in my bag," I mutter, and Evan laughs again, earning us both another throat clearing.

"You should have seen her the first day I came in here," he says. "She walked around the room about eight hundred times. I guess maybe she thought I'd make a run for the shelves if she didn't."

"God forbid you venture near the magazines," I say, and he smiles at me again, another of those lethally gorgeous smiles. He has a tiny gap between his two front teeth, and I know this sounds crazy, but the sight of it flips my insides all around.

I am so in over my head, and the really scary part is that I like it.

We study for a while. Well, not really. I try, sort of, but by the time the librarian gets up and glances at us briefly before disappearing into the back, I've taken about half a page of notes, by which I mean I've copied about half a paragraph from the world history textbook into my notebook. I swirl my pen down the page and look up. He's looking at me again, and this time he doesn't look away. If I were capable of writing poetry—which I'm not—I would write a poem about this moment, about him looking at me. He looks at me like no one else ever has, in a way that makes me feel fluttery, shy. I take a deep breath.

"How's Mar—your mom?" The moment I say it, I wish I'd said something else because a shadow crosses his eyes.

"Okay. How's . . . ?" He gestures vaguely. I know who he's talking about.

"Fine, I guess. I don't see him much."

"Always out?" I hear Mary in that, in the arguments she and Dad used to have.

"Yeah, work keeps him, you know, busy."

"Work?" I definitely hear Mary now.

"Yeah, he actually gave up dating."

"Gave up dating?"

"Well, see—" I'm not quite sure how to proceed. "Okay. He had, like, three girlfriends after . . ." I trail off, not wanting to mention Mary right now. "Anyway, they all moved in, and there were these huge scenes when they moved out, and so I told him after the last one that if he wants to do it again, he's gotta wait till I'm in college."

Evan makes a very noncommittal noise, and then says, "Does he still design houses?"

"Yeah. Your mom?"

"Nurse."

I smile, thinking of how she used to fuss over Evan or me if we got sick. It was nice, having someone do that. "I bet she's great at it."

He nods. "She is. After—after all the stuff that happened, we moved to Florida, to live near my grandparents, and she got her associate's degree and worked for a hospital there. Then she got offered a job in Flemington—you know, over by the mountains, so we moved back. She decided to go for her bachelor's and did her first year there, then we moved to Suffolk for her second year because she got an even better job. When she graduated in the fall, she got a job offer at the new Hamilton hospital. We moved here the day after Christmas. Third time we've moved in the past three years."

"So this is your—"

"Third high school. And the only one where I have to take some stupid required class in World History in order to graduate, despite the fact that it's an elective."

"I know!" I say. "What is that? When I tried to get out of it, I asked about that. I mean, how can it be required and an elective?"

"That's what I asked too. I bet they told you the same thing they told me."

"It's required because you have to take it in order to graduate. It's an elective because it's a term class," we both say, and grin at each other. He starts to say something else and then looks at the clock.

"Shit, I gotta go," he says, and starts gathering his stuff up.

I wait a couple of seconds, but he doesn't offer me a ride. I look down at my notebook and hope my face isn't as red as it feels. Just when I think I understand guys, I realize I don't understand them at all. I wish I could say something, even a simple "See you later," but all my words feel stuck in my throat. I figure I just won't look up, like I don't care that he's leaving.

He's got all his stuff, but he hasn't left because I can still see his sneakers as I sit there pretending to look at my notebook. I'm thinking maybe he wants me to grab my stuff and leave first, but there's no way I can do that since I don't have a way home and have to wait till after he goes to call Katie to see if she can come get me. I finally look up, and he's standing there looking at me, the strangest expression on his face, like he knows he should do something but can't help but do something else. When he sees that I'm looking at him, he looks away, staring down at the floor and running a hand through his hair. His fingers are shaking a little. "Do you—do you want a ride home? Or are you waiting for someone?"

"Let me just get my stuff," I say, and the expression on his face changes, that smile, the real one, returning, and have I mentioned that I'm in over my head? Because I am. I really, really am.

seven

On the drive to my house Evan is quiet and keeps looking at the clock. I wonder what happened to the guy I was laughing with just a few minutes ago, wonder what made him get so quiet, look so worried. I shift a little in my seat as we turn onto my street and feel a piece of paper crinkle under my foot. I look down at it. It says SAFETY NOTICE in huge letters, and the sentence below it says ANDERSON FREIGHT VALUES YOU, THE WORKER!

"Are you late to work?" I ask.

"A little. They offered me extra hours this week, and I can take them so . . ."

"I'm sorry," I say. "You didn't have to drive me home."

"I know. I wanted to."

He wanted to. I may be sitting in his car, but really, I'm floating. And then we're at the end of my driveway, and he's stopped the car and I should get my stuff. Except I'm not. I'm just sitting there, making him later because I don't want to go. I see him glance at the clock again, quickly, and I say, "Sorry," once more, embarrassed, and start gathering up my stuff.

He says, "Lauren," touching my wrist, and I freeze, look at him. He's looking at me. His eyes are so brown they look almost black, and the look in them makes my breath catch. He's leaning in a little, moving closer, and I want him to kiss me.

I want him to kiss me so much that I feel like everything else has faded away, that he and I are the only two people in the world. I'm in the kind of moment I've always wondered about and assumed was never real, something that just happened in books or on television or in movies. I never knew there could really be a moment where you know something is going to happen and you're just waiting for it, every thought you have focused on what you want to be real, on hoping—

"Someone's in your driveway," Evan says, surprise in his voice, and I look, see Katie's car. She's sitting on the steps, shading her eyes with one hand and looking down at Evan's car. At me in Evan's car.

I look back at him and say, "Thanks again for the ride," but the moment is totally gone, and we both know it because the smile he gives me is the quick chewed-off one from before, a little bitter and mostly not real at all, and his "Sure, no problem," is polite and nothing more.

I get out of the car and head toward Katie.

"Who was that?" she asks as I'm walking up the driveway.

"Guy in Axel's class. Have you been here long?"

"You're talking really fast," she says, "which means you don't want me to ask who drove you home. Which means—oh my god, tell me you did not get in a car with Jack Harris!"

I roll my eyes at her. "Yes. We stopped and robbed a bank along the way. Can I hide a bag of money in your car?"

She laughs and we go inside. I don't turn around to watch Evan's car drive away, even though I want to.

As I'm getting ready to go out with Dave, I keep thinking about Evan. I keep thinking about the two of us in the car, about him saying my name. Katie's talking, but I'm not hearing a word she's saying.

She flops across on my bed as I'm washing my face, and just when I'm splashing water around, trying not to get soap in my eyes, she says, "So who drove you home?"

"Can you get me a towel?" I ask, staring down into my sink. I hear her get up, and I hold my hand out for a towel. She passes me one, and I say, "Just a guy," drying my face extra carefully. "Evan."

"Evan Kirkland?" Katie's voice is surprisingly sharp, and I put down the towel and look at her.

"Yeah. You know him?"

"Not really. Marcus does, though. Did you and Evan talk about him?"

"The whole time," I say, and toss my towel at her. I wonder if Marcus was the person Evan was talking to earlier today.

I didn't know they knew each other. "Why would we talk about Marcus?"

She bats my towel away and looks relieved. "I just figured he'd be the one person you guys both know so . . . you know. I mean, what else do you have in common?"

"Well, sorry to break it to you, but not one mention of Marcus. I suppose I could bring him up next time, if you want."

"Next time? Did Axel assign you to a study group or something?"

I open my closet and look at my clothes. "Sort of. What shirt should I wear?"

She doesn't say anything and I turn around to look at her, wondering if she knows what—who—I'm thinking about. But she's not even looking at me; she's staring out the window.

"Hey," I say lightly. "Are you all right?"

"I'm worried about Marcus," she says, and I say, "What's going on?" and turn back to the closet with a little sigh. I should have known. Katie never comes over in the afternoon anymore unless she wants to talk about Marcus. Not that she came over a lot before, but at least before Marcus we would sometimes talk about other things.

I grab a blue shirt, unbuttoning the one I have on. As I take it off, I think about Evan's hand holding mine, about him looking at my fingers and asking if I was okay. I actually have a little bruise on the back of my hand now, a smaller, fainter twin to the one he has. I trace a finger across it and think about how I touched him the same way.

"So do you think he has a chance?"

"Absolutely," I say, even though I haven't been listening and don't know what she's talking about. Chances are it's still Marcus, though. I quickly shrug on the blue shirt. "Why wouldn't he?"

"It's just that he really wants to go to a good school."

I knew it was still about him. "Marcus not go to a good school? Come on. It's Marcus. He plays football—at the end of the season wasn't he the team leader in rushing or something?—plus he's a math genius. He'll be able to go anywhere he wants."

"He needs a scholarship."

I laugh. "Sure he does. Because really smart athletes are so often overlooked by universities."

"Lauren," she says. "He needs a full scholarship."

I turn around and look at her. She isn't kidding. I thought his family was like Dave's, comfortable in a comfortable house, but now that I think about it, Katie's only ever mentioned his mom. And I've never been to his house.

"He'll get one," I say, and start to brush my hair. "If not for football, then for the math genius thing. And didn't you say he got a perfect score when he took a practice SAT?" I know he did. She talked about it for two weeks straight. "He'll probably get a hundred full scholarship offers."

She nods and walks over to me, takes the brush out of my hands, and starts pulling my hair back and putting it up into this cool-looking loose ponytail.

"Yeah," she says, "and then he'll go to school a million miles away while I'll be stuck here, probably going to community college, so . . ." She trails off, tucks a strand of hair behind my ear, and steps back.

"You're a miracle worker," I tell her, and she smiles a little. "And besides, if anyone's going to end up in community college, it'll be me. Your grades are better than mine, and God knows your SATs will be. And to top it all off, you're a genius with hair. I mean"—I point at myself in the mirror—"it never does anything like this when I fix it. It just lies there like a lump. You and Marcus are going to end up going to the same school, and you're going to be so disgustingly happy that you'll make everyone sick."

"Sick," she says softly, a strange note in her voice, and then, seeing me looking at her in the mirror, waves a hand in front of her face. "Sorry, I didn't mean to go on like that. Things have just been kind of crazy at home lately."

Something tells me that's an understatement, and it makes me stop and look at her, wondering if everything's okay. "Crazy how?"

"Oh," she says, "you know," and goes over to my closet. She starts fiddling with my shirts, rearranging them by color. I try to catch her eye, but can't.

"Is it the birthday party thing?" I say, but she still won't look at me. I glance at my face in the mirror and try to decide if I should wear blush or not. I wonder what Evan would think of my hair like this.

"Pretty much," she says. "You must be thinking about Dave."

"What?" For a second I don't even know who she's

talking about, and then, oh yeah, Dave. My boyfriend.

"Your face is red," she says. "Tell me everything."

Okay, let's see. How would this sound? Katie, I actually forgot all about Dave. I've spent the past couple of days thinking about someone else pretty much nonstop. I totally ditched you today so I could sit in the school library and talk to him. Does that make me a bad friend to you, a bad girlfriend, or just really pathetic? Or maybe all three?

"You've painted your nails again," I say instead, getting up and moving her away from my shirts. "How do you do it?"

"Do what?"

"Paint your nails at five in the morning."

She shrugs. "It's the only time I can do it. Besides, we're all early risers at my house."

I know that's not true. Every time I've stayed at Katie's, her dad, who is a lobbyist, has never been home and her mom has been in bed. Katie says her mom is sick a lot, but doesn't like to talk about it, and I never know what to say when it comes to mothers anyway. The only people who actually do get up early are her brothers because they are addicted to cartoons. They get up at six every morning. Even on the weekends.

"Wait, so you're saying the only chance you ever have to do stuff like paint your nails is before your brothers get up?"

"Pretty much."

"So you get up and then—" I stop for a second, look at her. I realize, suddenly, that Katie must be the one who gets them ready for school every morning.

"You do everything," I say slowly. "Get them up, get them

to school, pick them up after. And this party, you're not just going to it. You're planning it."

"Yeah," she says. "It wasn't so bad when they were younger, but now—I'm never having kids, Lauren. Not ever." She sits down on the bed, and for a second she looks so tired and so lost that it scares me. I sit down next to her, rest my head on her shoulder.

"I'm sorry. But you'll be in college soon and then—"

"Then I'll have to live at home," she says. "Someone has to take care of them, Lauren."

"It shouldn't be you."

"Yeah, well." She shrugs. "It is."

"Katie," I say, but she gets up, goes and looks out the window.

"Dave's here," she says, and when she looks back at me she's smiling her usual bright smile. I want to say something else, something that will help, but when I look at her I know, suddenly, that anything I say won't make a difference at all. That's the other thing those books always lie about. They always make everything okay in the end, but that's not how life works. There are some things that can't be fixed.

eight

Dave greets me with a quick kiss and a broad smile. "You look amazing," he says.

"Not my doing," I say, pointing at my hair. "Katie did all the hard work."

"Your hair always looks beautiful," he says, lightly touching the little strands that Katie somehow got to curl around my face, and then asks her if she wants to go to the game too. "We could call Marcus, ask him to meet us there," he says, and Katie wants to say yes, I can tell, but then she shakes her head.

"I can't," she says. "Dad's home right now, and I can't leave him alone with Harold and Gerald for too long. They've just discovered the joys of dropping their lizard in people's laps so . . ."

She laughs and Dave laughs, and just a few minutes ago I would have laughed too, except now I know she isn't joking. She has to go home because she has to take care of her brothers. Her dad and my dad should get together sometime. I bet they could share tips on how best to ignore their kids.

"I'll talk to you later," I tell her, and give her a quick hug. "Do you want me to come with you?" I whisper. "I could help out."

She pulls away and shakes her head. "Have a good time," she tells me. "I'll see you tomorrow." She waves at Dave and heads to her car.

"You ready?" Dave asks, and leans in, gives me another quick kiss. I look at his beautiful face and feel his lips brush across mine, and it's nice, it really is. Almost every girl I know—and heck, probably even some of the guys—would love to be exactly where I am right now.

"Yep," I say, and if it's so nice and I'm so lucky, then why don't I feel happier?

John's basketball game is being held at the high school. Normally all the youth league basketball games are at the rec center, but this is the championship game, so it's a really big deal. Dave tells me how excited John is, how he's been practicing extra every day.

"Pretty soon he'll have to start getting ready for summer training camp," he says. "I'm thinking of helping out this year. You could do it with me, if you wanted." He grins at me, so sweet, and I know a good girlfriend would, but the idea of spending my summer standing around outside watching little kids run around is just not my thing.

"I bet your mom really wants to help out."

"She does, but I know she'd love it if you wanted to do it too. And it would give you a chance to spend more time with her. She really likes you, Lauren. She said the other day that she thinks of you like family."

"Really?" I say, and when he nods I put my hand over his on the gearshift. My own mother couldn't be bothered to stick around, but Dave's mom thinks of me like family. And like Dave, she would never say something like that unless she meant it. "Maybe I will—"

Dave moves his hand out from under mine, presses a quick kiss to my fingers, and then returns them to my lap. "Gotta pay attention to traffic," he says with a grin, and I don't finish my sentence because it wouldn't be just a whole summer of me watching little kids. It would be a summer of doing that and having Dave always keeping distance between us.

I ask him if he'll get to coach John's team. He says, "Maybe," and launches into a complicated explanation of how the coaches are picked. I look out the window. It's dark now, and I can't see anything except for the headlights on passing cars. I think about calling Dad and telling him where I am, but I'll just get his voice mail and besides, I'll be home before he will. John's game will end at 8:30, and Dave will drop me off before he goes to meet John and his parents for ice cream. It's what they always do. Family tradition, his mom calls it.

The first time I went to Dave's house, I couldn't get over

the shelves of awards. They were everywhere; filling up the living room, lined up neatly in the hallway nestled with framed pictures of Dave and John smiling with their parents. I'd never seen anything like it. When I got home, I didn't bother trying to find any awards—the closest I've ever come to one of those is a ribbon I got for participating in the science fair when I was in seventh grade—but I did try to find a picture of me and Dad and Mom together, caught up in the idea of framing it and having something like what Dave and his family had.

The only picture I could find was taken when I was about two. Dad was holding me, and we were both smiling into the camera. Unfortunately, you couldn't really see us because the picture hadn't come out right, blurred by a finger smudging the lens. My mom took the picture—you can see the glint of her wedding ring—and that finger, that ghostly blur, is the closest thing I have to a family picture, to a moment where the three of us were together.

When Dave and I walk into the gym it's packed, filled with parents smiling at their kids and chatting with one another. This is going to sound crazy, but I just love seeing all the moms and dads so excited for their kids, so interested in watching them do something, even if it's play youth league basketball. I see John doing warm ups with his team, and he waves at us.

Dave's parents are there, of course, and we sit behind them. They ask me how school is going and seem genuinely interested in my answer. In the beginning, when Dave and I first started going out, I figured there had to be something wrong with his family. I thought maybe behind all the togetherness and pride over everything Dave and John did was something else. I even had this idea that Dave would tell me that he really hated sports and wanted to be, I don't know, an artist or something. But Dave really loves sports and his parents are—well, as perfect as he is, basically. They're always there, always supportive. When John misses a basket they clap just as hard as when he makes one, and even though his team is down by six points at halftime, they go tell him how proud they are of him.

"Your parents are so great," I tell Dave.

He grins at me. "You know, they think you're pretty great too. I'm going to go grab a soda and say hi to John. You want anything?"

I shake my head and watch him head down the bleachers. All my conversations with Dave are like this. Wonderful. Kind. Not really about anything. Dave and I talk, sure, but we don't actually talk. In all the time we've been dating, I've never told him about my mom leaving. I've just told him that my parents aren't married anymore. I haven't . . . I haven't wanted to tell him. I know he'd be understanding and sweet, but he'd also know the truth.

He'd know that I'm worth leaving.

I'm different when I'm with Dave. My life is simpler, better, and I'm a nice person, a person worth sticking around for. I'm someone who really likes washing dishes with his mom after Sunday dinner and who sits beside him in church. That person is the one who Dave loves. And it's not that I don't like who I am with him. I love the me I am with him. I'm the girl who has

Dave. I'm Lauren, Dave's girlfriend. I'm someone better than Lauren Smith, who no one noticed till Dave came along.

The thing is, that girl isn't me and I know it. But when I'm with him, I feel like I could be her. That if something in me was just—I don't know, shifted a little or something, smoothed down—people would think of me the way they think of Dave, and everything would always be perfect. I would be perfect.

On the way home, Dave tells me that he's thinking about not trying for a big college after all but going to a smaller one. A local one. "I've checked into their admissions requirements, and you could definitely get in. And they're only a few hours away, so we could come home every weekend."

Because I need more time by myself rattling around the house, I think. But I don't say that. I would never say that to Dave. Instead I say, "I think it sounds perfect for you."

"Just think about it," Dave says, and then, "I'm sorry. I don't mean to push you."

"You aren't." Dave never pushes for anything. I look out the window. I can see my house. It's dark. Dad isn't home yet.

"I love you," he says when he's stopped the car and given me two—always two, never more—kisses good night.

I get out of the car and wave good-bye. I think about what he said, those three words I was so crazy to hear from someone, anyone, and was lucky enough to hear from him. They don't really sound like anything.

nine

I fall asleep before Dad gets home, and when I get up he's already left for work, leaving me a scrawled note that says he'll be home early tonight and that he misses me.

He misses me. I'm not sure I believe it, but it's nice to read. I definitely don't believe he'll be home early—I know better—but I do dig through the stack of menus we keep by the phone and pull out the one for the Chinese place he likes. At the very least I can watch him eat egg drop soup—his favorite—before I go to bed.

I don't see Dave in the parking lot when Katie and I get to school, and surprisingly Marcus isn't there either.

"Where is he?" I ask Katie, and she shrugs, trying to keep a grin off her face. She and Marcus have this thing where he "surprises" her with flowers or something on one of their many anniversaries. They have about a million—their first kiss, their first date, something to do with some song—and since they started having sex about a month ago, my guess is now they have another one.

"I bet it's flowers," I tell her, and she laughs, smooths the front of her shirt. I see the cuffs have this cool embroidery on them, woven intertwined strands of—you guessed it—flowers. I remember looking at the shirt in the mall a couple of weeks ago. It cost more money than I could ever convince my dad to spend on anything with the possible exception of books for college.

"Nice shirt," I say, poking at the flowers.

She bats my hand away and grins at me. "What?"

"Oh, please, Miss I-Plan-Everything. He's so getting you flowers."

She grins at me again, and we walk into school.

Surprisingly, Marcus isn't lurking by the door with a bunch of roses. In fact, he's nowhere to be seen. Clara Wright passes by and flicks her head at us, an almost greeting, and says, "If you're looking for Marcus, I was just talking to him by his locker."

Beside me I can hear Katie's mouth fall open and then snap shut again. Stupid Clara. I know she did that on purpose. I can tell because she's smiling now, that totally angelic and yet totally cruel smile that's her trademark. Well, that and her perfect hair and perfect body and stream of followers that trail behind her.

I wish I could think of something cutting to say, something that would make Clara stop smiling and make all her little followers look at her like she's a loser, but I don't. Clara is an unstoppable force of nature that sweeps through the school, and looking at her I feel like a little kid. I feel like nothing. I know that even if I could think of something to say, I wouldn't, and she knows it too, her smile broadening a bit before she moves on down the hall.

Katie and I look at each other and sigh.

"I knew it," she finally says when we're crossing into the hall where our lockers are. "She wants him back."

"She doesn't want him back. She's just being Clara. And even if she did—which she doesn't—Marcus loves you. I mean, he never did stuff like this for Clara."

"Probably because she wouldn't let him."

"Oh, please. Clara not wanting presents is just—well, the universe would have to end. Remember when she stopped talking to Jenny Spritz for not giving her a nice enough birthday present?"

"Who could forget?"

"See?" I say. "So she's full of shit, and you should just ignore her."

"Right," Katie mumbles, but she's almost smiling. I reach over and tug on one of her shirt cuffs, and she does smile then. We cross into the hall where our lockers are, and sure enough Marcus is leaning against his talking to someone, a bouquet of flowers in his left hand.

"Told you," I tell her, and then I see who Marcus is talking to. Evan. Evan, who is leaning against Marcus's locker, looking a little sleepy, with his hair falling over his forehead and trailing down toward his eyes. He nods at whatever Marcus is saying and shoves his hair back with one hand. It falls right down again, and I am staring. I know I am.

I also am not walking because Katie says, "Come on, hurry up," and tugs on my arm, drawing me toward Marcus.

"Hey," she calls out, and Marcus turns around. He looks startled, but just for a second, and his smile as he watches Katie reach him is happy, if somehow still a little surprised.

"Hey," he says. "I was just coming to look for you." His smile broadens, his eyes light up, and he holds the flowers out to her. The gesture would look silly on anyone and does, in fact, look pretty silly on Marcus, but it looks kind of sweet too.

She gives him a look—the I-just-saw-Clara look—and he says, "Katie," softly, like it's the best word in the world.

Evan clears his throat, the chewed-off smile I recognize from the first day of Axel's class on his face. "I'll see you around," he says to Marcus before glancing at me briefly. I feel my face heat, and I look down at the ground. When I look up he's turned away, and his smile has faded altogether.

Katie, who has leaned in toward Marcus, a smile on her face as she traces the petals of one flower, glances at Evan. "Hey," she says.

"Hi," Evan replies.

"I'm Katie."

"Evan."

"Oh," she says, giving Marcus a look I can't read. "Nice to finally meet you." Marcus clears his throat, and it's suddenly all very awkward and I'm not sure why. Evan glances at me again. Should I go ahead and say hi? Or should I act like we've never met? Best to do what I always do and just keep my mouth shut.

But to my surprise I find myself saying, "Hey, Evan," in a voice that's only slightly squeakier than normal.

Evan looks at me, and I see surprise and something else in his eyes, something that makes me feel warm and giddy and so very in over my head yet again. "Hey." He's smiling again, a real smile this time, and once more it's like the whole world has faded away. It's the strangest thing. I really like it.

"So, these are really beautiful," Katie says, her voice a little louder than normal, and the world comes roaring back with a vengeance. I turn to see her holding the flowers and looking not at Marcus but at me, a strange expression on her face. I look away from Evan and pretend that I have to find something in my bag right now.

"I gotta go," Evan says. I look up to see him and Marcus do that nodding thing guys do before he heads off down the hall. And now it's just the three of us, and Katie is still looking at me kind of funny.

"Well," I say, "I'm sure you guys want some anniversary time or whatever," at the same time Katie says, "I'll walk you to your locker." She whispers something in Marcus's ear that makes him flush red and grin at her, and then she marches me down the hall.

"He was staring at you the whole time," she says.

"Who?"

She looks at me, both eyebrows raised.

"Oh, please. No one stares at me unless I'm with Dave."

She gives me another look. I tap her flowers and say, "You should put those in water or something. I promise I can open my own locker all by myself."

"Plus Dave's looking for you."

I glance down the hall, and sure enough, Dave is at his locker, talking to some freshman girl while looking around the hall. I watch the girl lean in toward Dave, smiling and trying to press her chest against his arm. Dave, predictably, looks uncomfortable and moves away but manages to smile back, and I can tell the smile has given the girl a crush that will last till she's forty or something. Poor thing. She has on a really cute skirt, though. I wonder where she got it. I ask Katie that and she gives me another look.

"You're never jealous," she says. "I mean, if anyone talked to Marcus like that . . . but you? It's like you don't even notice. You didn't even notice Dave till I told you he was looking for you. What's going on with you?"

"Nothing."

"Lauren," she says, but then the bell rings and we all have to head to class. Dave sees me and waves, looking sad. I wave back and hope I look sad too, but the truth is, I'm really not.

The truth is, I'm still thinking about Evan smiling at me.

My classes are all long and boring and exactly like they are every single day. Honestly, going to high school is just like having a job. You have to show up, you have to do your work, and you have to be around tons of idiots or mean people. Now that I think about it, it's worse than having a job. At least there you get paid.

But then I get to music. It starts off the way it always does, with Mr. Herrity leading us through warm ups and telling people that they're sharp or flat or giving them the dreaded clearly-you-haven't-been-practicing glare. We run through most of the stuff we're doing in jazz band after that, but he throws in a march and then the piece we've been playing, the one with the solo. I've been practicing it, and it's in me now. That's the thing with music. When you're playing something you like, that you feel inside you, after a while it's like it is you. You see the notes, and you don't even have to think about them. You just know them. You just know what to do.

When I'm done Mr. Herrity tells one of the drummers to sit down and stay away from the tympani. Then he looks at me and says, "Nice job. We'll add the piece to the concert list."

I have a solo. A solo. Mr. Herrity's still talking, but I'm not listening at all because I have a solo. A solo! I've never had one before. Granted, the concert he's talking about isn't that much of one—we just play at a nursing home, but still. I have a solo.

I float through the rest of class, and afterward, as I'm washing up in the bathroom, ignoring the evil eye some sophomore is giving me as she waits to try to get soda off her shirt, Gail comes up to me.

"Congratulations," she says, and when I see her smile in the mirror I can tell she knows exactly how I feel, that she knows what it's like to play a piece and have it be part of you. And before I know it I've turned around, soap still on my hands, and we're talking.

"You had a huge solo last year," I say. "Tell me everything. Were you really nervous? How much did you practice? Mr. Herrity doesn't decide to take pieces off the concert list once he's added them, right?"

"Wow, I had no idea you . . ." Gail says, and then trails off.

"What?"

"Could look so happy," she says. "I mean, not that you don't look happy and stuff normally. But—" She points at the mirror. I look and hardly recognize the person smiling back at me. I didn't know I could look so happy either.

"I've just never had a solo before," I say, and rinse the soap off my hands. "And I'm—" I bounce up and down on my toes like a little kid, and am horribly embarrassed.

But Gail is still smiling, still looking like she knows exactly how I feel, and all she says is, "You should have seen me the first time I got one. I actually stood up in class and . . ." She waves her arms around.

"I remember that," I say, laughing. "That was—God, was that in ninth grade?"

She nods.

"So you're a pro at this," I say. "Maybe we could get together and practice sometime."

"Sure," she says, looking surprised. The sophomore waiting for the sink rolls her eyes at me, and I roll mine back but move away, waving to Gail as I leave.

Katie is waiting for me in the hall. "You look happy. What's going on?"

"Well," I say, but then she makes a face and digs in her

purse, hands me a tin of mints. "Honestly, I don't know why you stay in that class. No one takes it, and plus whatever that smell is—"

"Reed," I say, and put a handful of mints in my mouth, silencing any further conversation. And then I'm off to world history.

I swallow the last of the mints Katie gave me as I walk into the room. Evan is already sitting down, looking at Jack Harris, who is leaning across two desks to talk to him.

"So, what, you're not going to do it?" Jack says. "What are you, some kind of loser?"

"Guess so," Evan says, sounding totally bored.

Jack looks like he wants to say something else, but Evan's lack of interest in his insult has thrown him, and I can practically see him trying to think of something to say and failing. Most people avoid Jack or are afraid of him, but Evan just doesn't care and it's obvious.

Axel comes clomping in then, and Jack and all his friends start shouting out names the way she does when she calls roll. Most everyone laughs except for Gail, who looks annoyed, and Evan, who is looking around the room, still looking bored. When our eyes meet, he smiles a little.

I smile back.

Axel waits till Jack and his friends are done hollering, not looking upset at all, and then says, "Mr. Harris, Mr. Muntz, Mr. Ginson, and Mr. Dryson, thank you for allowing me to dispense with roll call. I also appreciate your interest in names. In fact, to recognize that interest, tomorrow you will all give individual oral reports on rulers of the Egyptian dynasties we've been talking about. Five minutes each, although you can go longer if you'd like. And should you not do the assignment, or fail to give a proper report—well, I think in that case I'll have to expect a ten-page paper from each of you on the subject by Monday. And, of course, failure to do the assignment by one of you—since you all clearly work so well together—will result in a failing grade for each of you. And as I know that Mr. Muntz and Mr. Dryson are hoping to graduate, I am quite sure you will all work very hard to make sure that they aren't held back just to repeat this class again."

"Bullshit," Jack Harris says, and Axel smiles at him.

"You're more than welcome to discuss your assignment with the administration if you wish," she says. "And if you say anything else like that during class today, I'll have you, Mr. Muntz, Mr. Ginson, and Mr. Dryson present reports *and* write papers. Now, where were we? Oh yes. Please turn to page . . ."

Jack Harris doesn't talk during the rest of class, and from the way Dryson and Muntz are looking at him, chances are he'll show up with a black eye or more tomorrow. Axel talks about Egypt, and while she might be the only person who can handle teaching the remedial history classes, she's a really boring teacher. I glance over at Evan. He's leaning back in his seat, eyes closed, but when she scrapes chalk across the board—I am convinced she does it on purpose—he opens his eyes and looks over at me. We share another smile, and I find myself wishing I had practice today.

And then thinking maybe it's a good thing I don't.

ten

Katie and Marcus drive me home after school. Clearly the anniversary I thought they were celebrating this morning is the one they are because they make out at every traffic light, and when Katie says she has to pick her brothers up by five, Marcus drives about a hundred miles an hour.

"I'll call you," Katie says as I'm getting out of the car, and before I can say anything, Marcus is whipping the car back down the driveway. I think about how annoying they are as I let myself into the house, but that's not really what's bothering me and I know it. I mean, they can be annoying, so cute I want to vomit, and I think I might have whiplash from the way Marcus took that last turn, but it's more than that. It's—I'm jealous. Not about Katie having Marcus or anything like that, just that they so obviously want to be together. As much as Dave likes—loves—me, he'd never act like that, never act as if nothing mattered but us being together. And I'm not sure I would either. When we first started going out I wanted to be with him all the time, but to be honest it was mostly because I was sure he'd dump me, and I figured if we were together a lot he'd do it quicker, that I wouldn't have to sit around waiting and wondering when he was going to wake up and realize he could do better than me.

But that's not how things worked out, and if Dave and I aren't like Katie and Marcus, that's okay. After all, didn't he just spend last night telling me that he's thinking about going to college around here and that he looked into it for me too? That's wanting to be with me. That makes me lucky.

"Very lucky," I tell myself, and I almost sound like I believe it. I put my stuff down and check the answering machine. Sure enough, it's blinking, and after two messages for Dad from some siding company that thinks calling him at home means they'll get a meeting sooner (shows how much they know), the message I knew was coming plays. Dad's voice, apologetic and distracted. He's running late, he's really sorry. "Go ahead and eat dinner, and we'll catch up when I get home."

"Sure we will," I mutter, but then I catch sight of my clarinet case and remember I have a solo. A solo!

I practice for a while, and by the time I order dinner I'm in a great mood. I call the Chinese place Dad loves and even order an extra egg roll for him to eat along with his soup. I eat dinner while I try to read a chapter of the book I'm supposed to be reading for English class, giving up when I realize I've dribbled lo mein everywhere and that my notes in the margin look suspiciously like a name that isn't mine or Dave's. I sigh and close the book, deciding to watch television for a while.

I really do wish I'd had practice today. I wish Evan had driven me home because today Katie wouldn't have been here, waiting, and—well. I clean up, turning off the television and tossing out the little packets of sauce that came with the food (we already have drawers full of them), and all the while I'm thinking about Evan and what it would be like to kiss him. The phone rings as I'm standing there thinking about being in his car and watching him lean toward me, close enough for me to reach up and touch his hair, and I actually let out a little shriek, I was so lost in thought. The answering machine clicks on as I'm heading for the phone, and I hear Katie's voice saying, "Lauren, I tried your cell but it's off. You never told me what was going on with you earlier today. Are you there?" There's silence for a moment, and I can hear her brothers in the background. Then her voice comes back again, tired and rushed. "Call me when you get a chance, okay?"

I don't call her. I think about it, and I mean to, but I end up straightening up the house instead. We have a cleaning service come in once a week, but Dad likes everything to be in a specific place, so I have to go through after they've come to make sure all the piles of stuff in his study are exactly where he left them, and by the time I'm done I've forgotten all about calling Katie. Sort of.

The truth is, I don't want to call Katie. I can't tell her about the solo—she doesn't even get why I take music—and I definitely don't want to talk to her about Evan. Not that there's anything to tell, really, but I can guess what she'd say if I even mentioned him. I saw her face when I got out of Evan's car yesterday. I saw how she was looking at me after I said hi to him this morning. Evan isn't popular. He isn't Marcus's friend. Dave is a great boyfriend, and everyone knows who I am because I'm the one girl Dave started dating and kept dating. Katie would remind me of all of that. She wouldn't say that I'm lucky, but we both know that I am and that girls like me don't give up a guy like Dave. Girls like me aren't even supposed to have guys like Dave.

I do some more homework, and then check my e-mail. Just the usual stuff—reminders from the school about a cheerleader charity bake sale. I send Katie a message, tell her I'm sorry I haven't called and ask if she thinks the "charity" part of the bake sale is about sending Clara and her followers to a cheerleading competition. Then I send her an e-card for her and Marcus's "anniversary." Just as I'm getting ready to sign off, I get another message.

It's from Dave. His mom has to work late tomorrow, so they won't be leaving for their family thing till Saturday morning. There's a dinner and a talk at his church tomorrow night, and do I want to come? "It would be great if you did. I really want to spend more time with you, plus everyone was so happy to see you at the holiday service and said they missed seeing you on Sundays. I love you!"

I think about deleting the message. Not replying, just deleting. I feel—I don't feel much of anything. But I should.

Dave wants to see me. People in his church, people he looks up to, want to see me. That's a good thing. I still don't reply to his e-mail. What's wrong with me?

I think about that while I finish my homework and watch a movie. The Sunday thing makes me feel a little guilty. I like Dave's church. I went every week with him and his family for a while, but found I missed going to church with Dad, even though it's mostly about him going around shaking hands and talking to people about whatever housing development he's working on. But it's still time with him, and Dave (of course) totally understood when I told him. He said, "Please tell your father I know how important this must be to him." I didn't bother to explain that it was actually more important to me.

Dad comes home as the movie ends, calling my name as he enters the kitchen.

"In here, Dad," I say, and he comes into the living room and smiles tiredly at me.

"I really did mean to be home sooner."

"I got you some soup. Sit down and I'll heat it up."

He's actually awake when I get back, smiles again at me when I pass him the soup. "Thanks, honey."

"Sure. I got you an egg roll too, if you want."

"Maybe later. One of the vendors ordered pizza, so . . ."

So I ate alone and he worked. Typical. "Sounds nice."

"I am sorry."

"I know."

Dad clears his throat, eats some soup, and then clears his throat again. "Did you have a good day?"

I think about telling him about the solo, but when I look over at him he's rubbing his head the way he does when he's got a deadline coming, and I know what he wants to hear. What I always say.

"Fine," I say. "It was fine."

Before I go to bed, I reply to Dave's e-mail. I tell him I can't go.

eleven

Evan isn't in school the next day. I notice in the morning as Katie and I are standing by our lockers talking to Marcus and Dave because he doesn't walk by, and when I look around I don't see him anywhere. I wonder where his locker is. It's probably at the far end of the hall by the door, where all the new kids get stuck with lockers, but still. I wish I knew.

"Who are you looking for?" Katie asks right before the first bell rings. As it does I tell her, "Clara," grinning when she rolls her eyes at me.

Dave says he got my e-mail when he's walking me to class. "I'm really going to miss you this weekend," he says, and I stand there looking at him, this amazing guy who is not only popular and smart but really kind, truly good in a way I didn't know people could be and realize I'm not going to miss him at all. I'm awful. Dave could be with anyone, and he wants to be with me. Me. I didn't understand why when we first started dating and, to be honest, I still don't. I've never asked him about it, though. There are a lot of things Dave and I just don't talk about.

"I'm going to miss you too," I say, and he gives me a quick kiss and then waves as he walks down the hall.

I find myself looking for Evan the rest of the day, watching people as I pass them in the hallway. I even hang around the cafeteria as lunch ends, thinking maybe I'll catch a glimpse of him.

I don't, and he isn't in world history. Jack and his friends have to give reports, and the period drags by. I keep looking at Evan's empty chair, wondering where he is. By the time class is over, I'm in a bad mood. I meet Katie and Marcus and Dave in the parking lot, and we divide off into our little groups of two. I see people walk by and look at us, and I'm suddenly sick of it—sick of school, sick of standing here, sick of everything. I just want to go home. I pull away from Dave.

"Lauren?" he says, concern in his voice, and puts an arm around my shoulder. It feels like a weight, pressing me down.

"I'm fine," I say sharply, and start to pull away again, but see Katie's eyes go wide and Marcus's narrow just a bit.

"I'm sorry," I say, and now I sound the way I always do around Dave—sweet and happy. "I just—my dad is being an ass. He found out about the sweater I got at the mall last month—Katie, you remember, the pink one?—and totally freaked out. I got a message from him last period telling me I can't go anywhere this weekend."

"But what about tomorrow?" Katie asks, and I shake my head.

"Sorry."

Katie looks pissed off, hurt even, and—damn. I forgot I'd promised to go to some party with her and Marcus, and now she's mad at me. Great. Just great. Sometimes I feel like all I do is annoy her.

"Sorry," I mumble again. She doesn't look any happier.

"Don't look so upset," Dave says to me, the arm around my shoulders pulling me closer. "Things will work out with you and your dad, and we'll just do something special next weekend." His eyes sparkle, bluer than the sky, and it sounds great, but I know that Dave's something special will involve me and either his church or his family, which is what we do every weekend. The last time we went on an actual date was—God, it was that party, *the* party, the one where I thought for sure we were over only it turned out we weren't. The party where Dave opened up to me, every girl's fantasy, and I sat there trying to figure out what to do.

I still don't think I know.

"I gotta go," he says. "Coach has me on this new training schedule and it's a killer." He gives me another quick kiss before he heads across the parking lot.

"So . . ." Marcus says to Katie, pulling her close, "what are you up to now?" and from the tone of his voice I can tell he's already forgotten I'm there.

Katie, thankfully, hasn't. "I have to give Lauren a ride home," she says. I try to ignore the way "Lauren" sounds clipped and angry. "And Harold and Gerald have to be picked up early today."

"Tonight?"

Katie shakes her head. "Dad left last night and I have to take Harold and Gerald shopping for their party because Mom's too busy."

That sounds a little weird because Katie never talks about her mom doing anything. In fact, the last time I saw her mom, I didn't even actually see her. She was in her bedroom, the door closed, and Katie knocked and said, "I'm home." There was no reply, and after a few moments Katie opened the door, went inside, and closed it before I could see more than that the room was dark, the only light a television flickering in the corner. When Katie came back, she had a tray full of dirty dishes and a sad almost-smile on her face. "Mom says hi," she said, in a whispery beaten voice, and I didn't say anything. I wish now I had. I wish I wasn't always letting Katie down. I wish I was a better person.

"I can call you though, right?" Marcus asks, and then he kisses her and the two of them disappear into each other the way all couples do. I look at my feet and try to imagine Dave kissing me like that. I end up thinking about Evan instead.

Maybe Marcus knows where he is.

"Hey, Marcus," I say, nudging his foot with my own. He pulls away from Katie and glances at me with a distracted look on his face. "Have you seen Evan today?"

"Who?"

"You know, the guy you were talking to yesterday morning."

"Oh, Evan," he says. "No, I haven't seen him today."

Katie shoots me a glance, impossible to read, but then Marcus turns back to her and they make out till Dave and a couple of other guys bellow his name from the direction of the gym.

"We should go," Katie says, and I think, *Thank goodness,* and start to get in the car.

They say their good-byes again after we get in the car, Katie leaning over me to talk to Marcus out my window.

"Bye, Marcus," I say when they're finally done, nudging Katie so she'll stop digging her elbows into my legs. Marcus looks at me, frowning a little.

"See you, Lauren," he says, but I get the feeling there's something else he wants to say.

"So it sucks, your dad grounding you over the sweater," Katie says on the way home.

I shrug. "You know how he is."

Katie fiddles with her CD player. "Kind of funny how the last time he grounded you was the time you and Dave were supposed to go away for the weekend."

"Yeah, well . . ." God, that. Our weekend together was actually a weekend of me, Dave, his family, and oh yeah, about four thousand other people at a family reunion. I had backed out at the last second, claiming to be grounded, but the truth was the thought of a whole family weekend scared and depressed me, made me long for something like that in my own family even knowing that if there was, it would never be like Dave's.

"Lauren," she says. "You've been really distracted, and just now with Dave, you seemed a little upset. Are things okay with you guys? Because he really does love you. You know that, right?"

"I know he does," I say wearily, not wanting to hear more and afraid of what she'd say if I told her how I really felt. "Look, I'm sorry about before. I know you wanted me to go to that party with you and Marcus."

"It's not that. I mean, it is, because Clara's going to be there and everything, but—"

"Marcus won't even notice her. Especially if you wear that blue shirt."

Katie grins, and I can tell I've distracted her. Good. "That's exactly the one I'm going to wear. I can't wait to see his face when he picks me up."

"Wow. Your mom must really like Marcus. My dad wouldn't let me go anywhere with anyone in a shirt like that." If he happened to notice I was wearing it, that is.

"She doesn't know his name," Katie says. "Half the time I don't think she even knows mine. She's—it's like she's lost or something, and my dad . . . he's never home, and I don't think either of them even know I'm dating. But that doesn't matter. What matters is that things can't get worse. Not until Harold and Gerald are older."

"Katie—"

"Don't," she says tightly. "I'm used to it."

"That doesn't make it right," I say, and God, how useless am I? What I've said won't help at all and we both know it. I clear my throat. "Is there anything I can do? Do you need any help?"

"I'm fine," she says, and the way she says it chills me because I know all too well what it can mean. What it usually does mean.

We ride the rest of the way to my house in silence, and when I walk inside I'm surrounded by it. I ignore my homework—it will still be there tomorrow—but I do practice my clarinet for a while. As I'm cleaning it out and checking my reed, I hear the garage door open.

I go and look, hoping it hasn't broken again. It did about three months ago, and for two days, until Dad got a repair person to come, it opened and closed nonstop.

But the garage door isn't broken. Dad is home, and when he sees me staring at him in surprise he grins, holds up a pizza, and says, "Extra cheese and pepperoni, right?"

We eat dinner together for the first time in I don't know how long. We even talk a little. I learn that Dad's latest housing project has run into some problems, something with zoning or variances. I tell him about my classes, and even get him to laugh when I describe Axel.

"So what else is going on?" he asks, and I actually start to tell him about the solo, but then his cell rings and he might as well be gone. I clean up the kitchen and put the rest of the pizza in the fridge. He gets up when I start the dishwasher, giving me a distracted smile as he heads to his study talking about layouts and tile sizes.

I go up to my room. I think about slamming my door, but there's no point. Dad wouldn't even notice. I look up Evan's name in the phone book and then online, but either his phone number isn't listed or Mary's last name has changed because I can't find anything. I wonder what he's doing now. If maybe there's a chance he's thinking about me.

I hear the doorbell ring and roll my eyes, get up, and shut my bedroom door. When a project is taking up all Dad's time—which most of them do—he usually has people come by the house on the weekend to work on plans or drop off stuff or "discuss strategy." I start to make a grocery list and try not to think about the fact that I'm seventeen and home on Friday night. The fact that it's by choice doesn't really make it better. It just makes me weird. Weird and a bad girlfriend and . . .

"Lee Lee!"

I ignore Dad and carefully write "coffee" on the grocery list. I really wish he'd stop calling me that.

"Lee Lee?" He sounds a lot closer now. Like he's upstairs or something, even. Huh. I write down "orange juice" and then cross it out. I'm always buying it and thinking I'll drink it in the mornings, but I never do.

"Lee Lee?" He really is upstairs, because he's actually knocking on my door. I get up and open it, wondering what's going on. He looks annoyed, the phone still attached to his ear. He's got a hand over the speaker.

"Someone's here to see you," he says, and then "Right, right," into the phone.

"Here? To see me?" Evan is my first thought and it's crazy, I know it. Why would he come see me? But still I'm dashing over to my dresser to look in the mirror to check my hair.

"Downstairs," my father says, hand over the receiver again, a puzzled look on his face as he watches me try to make my hair look decent. He says, "Yes, absolutely," into the phone, and then puts a hand over it again and says, "Your boyfriend. Danny?"

Not Evan. I stop messing with my hair. "Dave," I say, and push past my father, heading downstairs.

It is Dave. He's standing in the front hallway, looking a little uncomfortable. "I think I disturbed your father," he tells me. "Is he mad?"

I shake my head. Dad comes wandering back downstairs, still on the phone. When he reaches Dave and me he says, "Hold on a second," and actually stops talking on the phone.

"Very nice to meet you," he says to Dave, and the two of them shake hands. I think about reminding Dad that he's met Dave before—twice—but decide it isn't worth it. Dave, perfectly polite as always, shakes his hand and says, "You too, sir," with a slightly puzzled look on his face.

Dad nods, starts talking on the phone again. Before he shuts his study door he says, "Have a good time," the last word cut off by the snick of the door closing.

"Sorry," I tell Dave. "He's just really distracted. Big thing at work. You know how it is."

Dave nods, and I bet he thinks he does but he doesn't. He so doesn't.

"The speaker at church wasn't able to come because she missed her plane," he says, "and so I thought I'd come by and surprise you. Are you surprised?"

"Very," I say, and give him a quick kiss. "Come on upstairs."

Dave actually takes a step back. "Upstairs?"

"Yeah, I'm making a grocery list," I tell him, grinning. "You can help."

"I—" he says. "Your dad—"

Won't care, I want to say. Won't even notice. "We'll leave the door open so he won't worry and can do the check-up thing."

"Okay," Dave says, and we go upstairs.

Where we actually work on the grocery list.

It isn't that bad, actually. He's good at thinking of things that can be made quickly—he tells me about this dish that involves peanut butter and spaghetti, which sounds like an odd combination but less so as he explains the recipe.

"You know everything," I say, writing down "peanut butter" and scooting a little closer to him on the bed so our shoulders touch.

He laughs and doesn't even move away, actually leans over and kisses me. I look at his closed eyes for a moment before I close my own. We kiss for a few minutes, and he's holding me tight, one hand sliding under my shirt to stroke my back. And then he pulls away, his face flushed and gives me a look I know so well, one that says that while he might still want to kiss me, he's not going to. I fiddle with the shopping list, writing "bread" on it in heavy strokes. Under it I write "jelly" even harder, so that the pen pushes through the paper.

"Lauren? Are you all right?"

I look over at Dave. He looks so sweet and concerned, and how great is it that I have a boyfriend who respects me? Who doesn't push me? Who's happy to sit around and help write up a grocery list? Heck, who does all that and even knows recipes a cooking idiot like myself can make?

It's not great at all. It should be, but it isn't. I'm tired of perfection. I put down the list.

"Why don't you want to kiss me?"

Dave looks like I've hit him. "Lauren," he says. "Of course I want to kiss you. I want—I care about you. But your dad, he's—"

"Downstairs and totally oblivious. And even if he wasn't, we were just kissing, Dave."

Dave shifts a little on the bed, looking at me, and I move toward him. He doesn't move away, and up close he's even better looking, which doesn't seem possible but yet somehow is true, and we kiss again. This time he doesn't pull away and even moves closer, one hand curling around my waist.

And it's nice, really nice. I feel safe like this, Dave's mouth pressed against mine. It's familiar.

It's boring.

Did I just think that? Dave moves his mouth a little, and I did think it. I'm still thinking it.

I'm a freak. How can I be bored kissing Dave? Right now, I'm kissing him. I shouldn't be bored. I wonder what it would be like to kiss Evan. I try to picture it, Evan here, in my room, and suddenly I'm a lot less bored, Dave's mouth somehow suddenly different, better. More exciting.

Oh.

I shouldn't be thinking about Evan. Not like that and especially not now. But I do, and when Dave finally pulls away, looking a little dazed and saying we really should stop, I let him go. I walk him downstairs, listen to him tell me he loves me, listen to myself say that I love him in return. I wave as he gets in his car, and I'm not thinking about him at all. I'm thinking about Evan.

I'm attracted to Evan. The thing is, I'm not sure what to do about it. I mean, I've liked guys before, tons of times, but not like this, this almost sick hot flutter in my stomach, like a second heart. I don't feel bored. I don't feel safe. I lean back against the door and try to think about Dave, but my head is full of Evan, of how he talks, how he looks. Of worry that I won't see him again. Of worry that I will.

"Lauren?"

I open my eyes and Dad is standing in the hallway looking at me. He looks very uncomfortable.

"Dave just left," I tell him.

If anything, saying that seems to make him even more uncomfortable. He shifts his weight from one foot to another, looks down at the floor.

"Dad?" I say.

"Are you being careful?" His voice is very quiet, almost a whisper.

"Dad!"

"Lauren," he says, and I hear fear thick in his voice.

"You have nothing to worry about," I tell him, and kiss him good night. I go upstairs and get ready for bed. After I turn out the lights, I lie there thinking about what happened tonight, about what my dad said. About what he meant.

About what he didn't say.

This was the sex talk my dad gave me:

When I was fifteen, I came down for breakfast one morning, and he'd left me a note that said "Doctor's appointment, 1 p.m. I'll pick you up." I figured it was for the dentist, but when he came to school and got me he took me to a gynecologist, and before I knew it my father was shaking the doctor's hand and saying, "Phil, how's that house working out for you?" and I was whisked into the back for an exam where I learned that stirrups weren't something that had to do with just horse riding. I was also given a safe sex pamphlet and a prescription for birth control pills.

"I don't understand," I said to Dad afterward, when we were driving home from the pharmacy and I was staring down at a little white bag containing a pink plastic circle full of tiny pills.

"I want you to be safe," he said. "I want you to have choices."

That shut me up, and I think he knew it would.

I wasn't planning on taking the pills—I hadn't even been

kissed, and the possibility of a boyfriend was, I was sure, an impossibility—but when I came down to grab breakfast the next morning, he was actually there. More than that, he'd even made breakfast. I sat down, stunned, and he passed me a plate of eggs and said, "Are you feeling okay?"

I looked at him and realized he wasn't mad at me, wasn't trying to hurt me. He'd meant what he'd said, and not in a bad way. He just meant it. He wanted me to be safe. To have choices. To not end up like him and Mom. I said I was fine, and when I went upstairs to grab my backpack, I took a pill.

twelve

The thing my dad has never said but that I've always known is that I was a mistake.

Dad was in college when he met my mom. Nineteen and determined to make a name for himself, he was the first person in his family to go to college. His parents hadn't wanted him to go, told him to turn down the scholarship he'd gotten and to join the army. Dad says they thought they were being practical. I couldn't tell you what my grandparents really thought because I've never met them. They don't talk to my father anymore, and haven't for years.

I'm the reason why.

Dad met Mom at a party. I only know that because I remember her saying it to my father once, something sharp and bitter in her voice, her hand resting gently on my head. "Remember when we met? I'd always thought parties were so much fun and then . . ."

Mom was eighteen, just getting ready to graduate from high school. She wasn't sad, wasn't messed up. She was perfect. I have her senior yearbook hidden in my closet, but I don't have to see it to tell you what her picture looked like, what was written below it. I memorized all of it a long time ago.

She's smiling in her picture, a beautiful sunny smile, and below her name is a list, a long list: Honor Society. Homecoming Court 9, 10, 11, 12. Homecoming Princess 9, 10, 11. Homecoming Queen, 12. Cheerleader 9, 10, 11, 12. Cheerleading Captain, 12. Blood Drive Coordinator. Student Council. It goes on and on. The next to last line is Most Beautiful. Right below that is Most Likely to Succeed.

She was going to go to Yale. I have the acceptance letter too, folded up and in its envelope inside the yearbook. On the envelope my mom has started to write a list of things she wants to take to college. The list stops halfway down, in the middle of a word. She was probably distracted by something and meant to finish it later, but part of me sees something else, sees my mother planning her future when suddenly she has to stop. She rushes to the bathroom, heaves up her insides. When she's done she looks in the mirror and knows she won't be finishing the list. She knows she won't be going to Yale. She'll have to settle for meeting me.

I know Mom and Dad met at a party, but I don't know how they met or what they talked about. I don't know if they liked each other or just happened to turn to each other by chance. I do know that they made me. And I know that when my father got back to school, he came home from classes one night and my mother was there, waiting for him. I sometimes wonder if he didn't know who she was, didn't remember her. Maybe he did and had been longing to see her again. I don't know. What I do know is she told him about me.

The next bit I know in my bones, a moment I was there for but can't recall because I was just a cluster of cells churning my mother's insides and changing her life. My dad sat down next to my mother and looked at her. He hadn't really looked at her before, and when he did, finally, he realized she was someone he could love. That maybe he already did love. He once reminded her of this moment, a little while before she left. I was playing with a doll and they were talking, their voices ringing from the room they were in to mine, wrapping around me.

"I fell in love with you that night," my father said. "You were so brave, so sure. You said you didn't want anything from me, that you just wanted me to know. I knew then that I couldn't let you go."

I don't know what my mother said to my father that long-ago night, but as I sat there holding my doll she said, "You should have."

He didn't, of course, and I think she must not have wanted him to. At least not then. She wanted to keep the baby. I know that because when she said she was pregnant and would be keeping the baby, her parents wept, begged her to think of her future, of all she had and could lose. She told me that, dreamy voiced as I sat in front of *Sesame Street* one afternoon. "But I made the right choice," she said, and pulled me into her arms. That was when I was very young, back when she was still almost happy with her life, with my father. With me.

Her parents suggested deferring Yale for a year, made gentle hints about how she needed to seize her opportunities. But there was a streak of something wild in my mother, and she said no. She turned Yale down, refused to go. Her parents were angry and, when that didn't move her, frightened. She left them, walked out of their house one day and never went back. They are another family I don't know, their story another one I can't tell.

She moved in with my father, and the morning he woke up because I was kicking, feet tenting against my mother, he asked her to marry him. She made him wild too, I guess, and so at nineteen, he found himself married with a baby on the way.

They were happy, though I can't really picture them that way. The woman I knew was quiet, always looking past me and my father to somewhere—anywhere—else. But she was happy, at least for a while, and so was my father. There are a handful of photos to prove it, the two of them smiling, standing framed under an arch somewhere, my father's hand resting gently on my mother's stomach. The two of them sitting together, arms around each other, not even noticing the camera because all they see is each other. The best picture, and the one I hardly ever look at, was taken just after I was born. They are in the hospital and my mother is laughing, her face turned toward my father, her eyes shining. My father is looking back at her, and I've never seen him look that way at anyone. I thought that with

Robin, his last girlfriend, maybe—but it never happened. I think he's afraid to let go like that. To feel like that. I really don't blame him.

There are a few more pictures after that, but the two of them are never together in them again. I enter them instead, and one of them is always holding me, the other person behind the camera, a ghost that can't be seen. There's one picture of us the day we moved into the house. Mom is holding me, gazing up at the sky. I am in her arms, my fingers wrapped in her hair as if I'm trying to pull her back down to earth. To get her to look at me.

I don't know exactly what went wrong, but I know things did. All my memories of us in this house are of quiet. My father being quiet when he came home, my mother staring out a window and nodding at everything I say before turning to look at me with a distracted look on her face. Eating dinner, the only sounds utensils being lifted and food being chewed. Her hands pressed against a window, and the look on her face when she turned and saw me.

I think love ate her up. I think all she had left was that wild streak, the one that had led her to my father, to me. I think it pointed her elsewhere and so she went.

She left when I was six. It was a Tuesday. I remember that. She waited for the bus with me in the morning just as she always did, stood silently drinking coffee and watching the road. She kissed me good-bye when the bus came, a quick brush of her lips across the top of my head. I pulled away and ran onto the bus because I knew she'd do it again tomorrow and the day after that and the day after that.

I wish she'd told me she wouldn't. I would have held still. I would have held her tight, trying to remember all I could.

When I got home the front door was unlocked. I didn't think anything of it; I thought she was outside, upstairs. I thought she was there because she always had been and because all I knew told me she always would be. I watched television, ate ice cream, all the things she was careful in allowing. I cried a little when it got dark, afraid she was lost, afraid I was somehow in the wrong house.

When Dad got home I remember he came in and called Mom's name, then mine. When I came out of the living room he said, "Honey, go wash your face," in a distracted voice. I did, and when I came out of the bathroom he wasn't there either. I ran through the house, ran upstairs. He was in their bedroom, staring inside their closet. All his stuff was there but hers was gone except for a neat packet of papers lying on a shelf. My dad picked it up, flipped through it. Put it back down. Later I realized the packet must have been divorce papers, prepared and signed and waiting only for him to see them, to scrawl his name across them and end their life together.

"She's gone," he said, and he sounded like I felt, lost. And then he turned to me and said, "Should we have pizza for dinner?" smiling broadly and too sunny, fake, and I knew what the empty space where her things used to be meant. I knew she had left and that she wasn't coming back. I just knew. I thought maybe I should cry, but I couldn't. I just kept staring at that empty space, staring until my father took my hand and led me downstairs, where we both acted as though everything was fine.

We never talked about it. I kept going to school, except now instead of waiting with my mother in the morning, I waited by myself, and after school I went with most of my classmates to a sunny place full of toys and an ever-changing array of faces. My dad started taking all his laundry and mine to the dry cleaners. When people began to ask questions my father simply said, "It's just Lauren and me now," and everyone nodded, smiled at me, or patted my head or pulled me into their arms as if their touches, their hugs, could somehow make everything all right.

I once asked if I could call her. My father put his head in his hands for a moment, and then looked back up at me.

"Lauren, honey," he said. "I don't know where she is."

No one did. No one does. I still don't know. I used to plot out adventures for her when I was younger, picture her as a spy, a waitress, a firefighter. I pictured her coming back with stories and presents. I pictured her pulling me into her arms and saying she was never leaving again, that she'd missed me every day, every second, that every breath she took reminded her of me.

Now I try not to think about her at all. She made her choice, and she didn't choose my dad. She didn't choose me. When I do think about her, I mostly think about how I might be like her. How there's a part of me that rises up, restless, from time to time. That thinks things I don't know how to handle, that makes me feel things I don't think I want to feel.

I think the way I feel when I look at Evan comes from her. In pictures taken the day she married my dad, she was reckless, laughing, spinning around in circles. She looked like her whole world was him. She looked a kind of happy I can't even imagine.

I don't want that. I don't want to be like that. I don't want to feel the way she did because I know what happens when you do. You love with your whole heart, with everything, and you wake up one morning and kiss someone good-bye the way you always do except you mean it as good-bye forever.

thirteen

I avoid Evan on Monday. And Tuesday. I don't look for him in the halls or the cafeteria. I stare at Axel in world history as if she's actually interesting, which is not an easy task. I skip jazz band practice, claiming I don't feel well, in order to catch a ride home with Katie even though the concert is this week and I know Mr. Herrity will be furious with me. I throw myself into what I have and stay close to Dave. I watch everyone watch him, their gazes flickering over me. I tell myself I am lucky. That I am happy.

Katie told me the party went fine, better than fine. Clara didn't even show up. She's very happy about that, and we're discussing it again (third time since Monday) as we're taking the long way to the parking lot, walking back through the school so Katie can "bump into" Marcus while he's standing around waiting to use the weight room. Since our football team actually had a winning season, Marcus has joined the wrestling team to keep in shape and so has to spend most of his afternoons either practicing or working out. As we pass the library, I see Evan heading inside.

The thing is, avoiding him has just made me think about him more. I couldn't tell you what I was supposed to have learned in any of my classes, even music. All I've been thinking about is not thinking about Evan.

He glances up as we walk by, and his eyes, dark and unsmiling, meet mine. I bite my lip and keep walking, keep silent. But I don't look away, even though I know I should, and have to fight the urge to turn around and keep looking after we pass by. And when Katie, as predicted, bumps into Marcus, I think about going back to the library. It would be easy enough. I'd just tell Katie I'd forgotten something, that I had another ride. She's distracted, probably wouldn't even listen. I could walk back to the library. I could walk over to Evan's table. I could say hi, ask if I could sit down. He'd look at me and I'd say—

"Hey, you." Dave's arms wrap around me, his chin grazing the top of my head. "What's going on?"

"The usual," I say, pointing at Katie and Marcus.

"Plus you wanted to see me, right?"

I tilt my head back and look at him. He's teasing, a gentle light in his eyes.

"Of course. And I bet you were out here waiting for me to walk by, right?"

"Hoping," he says, and he isn't teasing now, his voice low and worried. "Can—can we talk for a second?"

"Sure," I tell him, surprised by the request. Dave is always polite, of course, but this is extra polite, even for him. He looks worried too, his forehead scrunched up the way it gets when he has something to say that he feels bad about, and he's not really looking at me as we walk away from everyone else. I guess whatever he wants to say he doesn't want anyone else to hear. I wonder what it could be for a moment and then I realize.

He's dumping me.

The sad thing is I'm not upset. Not even a little bit. He and I have been together for more than a year, and now we're over and I . . . I'm thinking about Evan. I'm thinking that if this doesn't take long I can say I need time alone. I can wander back through the school. To the library.

Dave takes me outside, to one of the benches that people sit on when they have something to say that whoever is with them won't want to hear. We sit down and he won't quite look at me, instead stares at a place just over my left shoulder, as if he can't or doesn't want to really look at me. I fold my hands together and wait for him to talk.

Sometimes I would give anything to be a normal girl. To be the kind of girl who would sit here and feel what she's supposed to. I should be upset, I know it, but I'm not. I'm not the kind of girl I should be. I'm me, just me, and when Dave says, "Lauren, you know how sometimes something is really hard to say?" I lean over and take one of his hands in both of mine.

He doesn't speak so I say, "Dave, it's okay. Just tell me."

"It's my parents. They're driving me crazy." Wow, he sounds so sad, almost guilty. Maybe he's got someone else already and—Wait.

"Your parents?"

He nods. "They're worried I'm doing too much. Over the weekend they actually made me sit down and list everything I do, then said I don't take enough time to relax. I thought they understood me, but they don't. They don't get that this is what I want to do. They don't listen."

"Please," I say without thinking, my voice sharp, thrown by how disappointed I am that this was what he wanted to say. That he didn't want to break up with me. "They listen. They even care about what you're doing enough to want to make sure you aren't doing too much."

"But it's like they don't trust me."

"No. It's like they notice you, love you. You're lucky. You don't know how lucky—" I break off, look down at the ground. I don't want to talk about this. Not now. Not with Dave.

"Hey," he says, concern in his voice. "Are you all right?"

"I'm sorry," I say, forcing the words out, fighting to keep my voice level. I can't believe he didn't dump me. I can't believe how upset I am that he didn't, but I am. "I'm just tired or something. What are you going to do?"

"I don't know," he says, and leans over, cupping one hand under my chin and gently lifting my face up. "Talk to them, I guess. Tell my girlfriend I love her and think she's wonderful."

"I'm not wonderful."

"You're perfect," Dave says, and kisses me.

He doesn't know me at all.

The next day, as Katie and I are driving into the parking lot, she spots Marcus talking to someone. She slows down, rolls down her window, and calls Marcus's name. He turns and waves but doesn't walk toward us, just goes back to his conversation.

He's talking to Evan. And whatever they are talking about must be important because they are still talking when Katie and I are heading toward them. Right before we reach them I hear Marcus say something, but it's too quiet for me to hear. Evan shakes his head and looks past Marcus. Looks right at me.

I know I made avoidance plans and everything, but I don't care. He's standing there, his hair messy, dark, and gleaming even under the overcast sun, dressed in jeans splotched with what looks like paint or grease or both, bandages on the knuckles of two of his fingers. People walk by, pushing past him like they don't even notice him, and I don't get it. He's all I can see.

He smiles and I smile back.

Katie's arm knocks into mine. "Sorry," she says. "Dave's calling you."

I look around and see Dave standing inside a throng of people, all of them waiting for him to say something, to notice them. Dave's the female version of Clara—except that he's actually a nice person and doesn't even seem to notice how popular he is. I look around and realize almost everyone is watching him, as if whatever he says or does will be the most important thing anyone has ever heard or seen. I look back over at Evan.

He's still looking at me, and when our eyes meet again his grin gets a little sharper, a little more mocking, and I feel myself flush even though I don't know why I do. Marcus glances over at me, following Evan's gaze, and frowns a little.

"Bye!" Katie says, her voice bright in the way it gets when she's annoyed or worried or both. I look at her, and she looks pointedly at Dave.

"Bye," I say in return, wondering exactly what her problem is, and glance over at Evan again. He's gone now, walking into the school, and only Marcus is there, still looking at me with a small frown on his face. I head toward Dave.

Dave reports everything with his parents is fine and thanks me again. "You really reminded me of how great they are," he says as we're walking to my first class. "And what you said about how lucky I am? Dad said it sounded like something Mom would say to him when he's upset. He said we reminded him of how he and Mom were when they first got together and told me to make sure to hang on to you."

I wonder what Dave thought about that. I look at him, but I can't read anything in his face. He looks happy, just like he always does.

"Do you want to hang on to me?" I ask, and he blinks at me, like he's surprised by the question, and for a second, just a second, I think I see a shadow of something in his eyes. But then the bell rings and someone rushes past us, pushing him into me, and it's gone by the time he's pulled away.

After that it's pretty much a day like any other except that in second period I remember that the jazz band concert is today. I actually hadn't really forgotten it; I was just so freaked out (and okay, felt guilty about missing practice) that I thought I'd used up every single bit of worry last night, when I didn't fall asleep till after three. I guess I hadn't because I suddenly become convinced that I forgot to bring my clarinet to school even though I know I did. I raise my hand and ask to go to the bathroom, and after a lot of pleading, get a hall pass and head for my locker. I check and everything is fine. My reed is there, snug in its little case, and I even have two backups. Thank goodness. I go back to class in time for a pop quiz and the fact that I'm going to fail it is almost enough to take my mind off the concert. Almost.

I practiced my solo a lot over the weekend, but I missed the final practice and I know Mr. Herrity is angry with me about that. And sure enough, when I head toward music before lunch (the best thing about concerts, other than having a solo in one, is getting to leave school for a few hours) he pulls me aside and asks if I think I'm ready, "because if you haven't been practicing, it's better to tell me now than to wait and have everyone notice during the show."

"I'm ready," I tell him, and I am. Or at least I think I am.

We all shuffle onto the waiting bus, and as I walk on I realize I have to play the where-to-sit game. As much as I like jazz band, a lot of the people in it are people I don't know/don't talk to. I mean, as much as Katie harping on me about taking music is annoying, she is right that it's kind of a total loser thing. Then I see Gail sitting next to a window, the seat beside her empty, and feel relieved. If nothing else, we can talk about Axel.

"Hey," I say when I sit down, and she looks at me, startled. "Hey."

The bus lurches into gear, and we head away from the school. It's a relief to see the big painting of the school mascot, a blue and yellow otter, fade into the distance.

"I'm going to have nightmares about that otter when I'm in college," Gail mutters and I laugh, and before I know it, we're looking over the piece with my solo in it and I'm saying, "I'm just so nervous. What if I screw up?" It actually feels really nice to talk about stuff with someone instead of just letting all the worry sit inside me like a big cold knot.

"You won't screw up. And even if you do"—Gail lowers her voice, leaning in toward me—"there's no way you'll ever top Andy Plotnick."

We both giggle. Andy is the first chair trumpet player, and last year he had an entire solo piece which, the first and only time he ever played it in concert, he completely screwed up. Not only that, instead of continuing after his first missed note like a normal person would have, he stopped and said, "Wait, wait, let me start over." Everyone laughed—even Mr. Herrity, though he tried really hard not to show it—and for the rest of the year, any time anyone made a mistake in class we'd say, "Wait, wait, let me start over."

Someone calls out Gail's name in this weird, mean drawling way, laughing. Her face turns bright red, and I turn around to see who said it. It's Carl, one of the drummers, and when he sees me, he laughs even harder and says, "Dave Hall's girlfriend? Man, I'd love to see his face right about now."

"What's his problem?" I ask, turning back around and rolling my eyes at Gail. "I mean, besides all his usual ones."

I wait for her to laugh but she doesn't. She just shrugs, her face still bright red.

"Let me guess, he asked you out and you turned him down." Carl asks everyone out. In the days prior to Dave, I used to try to console myself with the fact that even if I'd never have a boyfriend, I'd at least been asked out. Though really, having Carl ask if you want to come over to his house to play some weird role-playing game and check out his room was more depressing than not having been asked out at all.

Gail grins at that, a little, but shakes her head.

"Oh, it's okay," I tell her. "Seriously. He does it to everyone and always acts like an ass afterward. You'd think he'd be used to rejection by now. Did you get the invite to 'check out his room'?"

"He didn't really say that. I mean, that's so stupid—" She sits up, looks back at Carl, and then at me. "He did say it, didn't he?"

I nod and she laughs, and the rest of the bus ride is fine. Fun, even.

The concert is . . . well, it's really pretty lame, just like I knew it would be. We play at a retirement home for a cluster of people sitting on the lawn, most of whom aren't looking at us at all and are instead staring up into the sky or at the ground.

But it's a beautiful day, and when I'm playing my solo I look out at old people and I feel good. It's not because I'm playing well, although miracle of miracles, I'm not doing bad at all. It's that I'm making them happy. I can see some of them nodding along to the music or tapping their feet, and a few of them are smiling. Music is doing that for them, and I'm part of that. It's an amazing feeling. I wonder if Evan would understand how I feel right now. I bet he would.

It's not until later, way later, on the bus ride back to school, that I think about Dave and realize I never thought about him while I was playing. Not once. I never even thought about telling him about my solo. It meant something to me, was important in a way most everything else isn't, but I didn't want to share it with him and know, somehow, that I won't.

fourteen

That night I call Dad. He doesn't answer, of course, so I leave him a voice mail telling him I'm going to study at the library with Katie. Right before I hang up I say I'm going to take the other car unless he calls and says I can't. I'll be gone by the time he listens to the message, so there will be no way he can yell at me for not asking permission. And besides, chances are he won't listen to the whole thing and will have no idea that I've gone out at all.

I go over to Katie's and pick her up, then drive her to the rec center where Marcus is waiting. He's not supposed to see her during the week; Marcus's mom is really strict, and although Katie goes over to his house after school she has to be gone before his mom gets home, and between that and her brothers, they don't really spend a lot of time together. Or so they claim. Anyway, Marcus is allowed to go to the rec center one school night every week to work out or play basketball or use the pool, and so he just says he's going there and then meets Katie.

I drive because Katie isn't allowed to drive anywhere on weeknights unless she's doing something family-related, and that always involves her brothers. Naturally, she doesn't want them around when she's with Marcus. So she says she's studying with me, I tell my dad I'm studying with her, and that way if Marcus's mom ever gets suspicious, Katie has a cover story in place. Not that it really matters, because in order for Marcus's mom to check to see if he's with Katie, she'd have to get Katie's mom to answer the phone, and the only person who ever checks our answering machine at home is me. Dad gets all his calls on his cell and doesn't really listen to any message that isn't work-related. I know that because I've done this one night every week for three weeks now, and he's never said anything despite the fact that I've left him a message about taking the car every single time.

After I leave Katie and Marcus, I head to the library. I've told Katie I go to the mall, but I always go to the library instead. I like the library, and I love going there on weeknights. It's quiet but not quiet like it is at my house, and if I don't like the book I'm reading, I have tons of others to choose from. Tonight I grab a copy of the novel we're supposed to be reading for English (unsurprisingly, they have plenty of copies of it) and then a book that actually looks interesting. One of the librarians I worked with the summer I met Katie stops by and asks how I'm doing and what colleges I'm thinking about applying to. That's another thing I like about the library. All the librarians know me and ask stuff like that—about my classes, about where I want to go to college. About me and how I'm doing. It drove Katie crazy when we worked here, the way they always asked how we were and stuff, but I liked it a lot. It wasn't like they were parents or teachers or anything, and asking because they were supposed to.

We talk about colleges for a while, and I get the names of a couple of small schools that sound like they might be worth looking into and that might actually take me. I read two chapters of the novel for English after that, and then I give up and start the other book I've grabbed. It's really good, and I read until another of the librarians comes by and tells me they're closing soon. I look at the clock, surprised. I hadn't realized it was so late. Usually Katie has called by now. I check my phone to make sure I have the ringer set on vibrate and not turned off, but it's fine and I don't have any messages. Great. I get that Katie wants to see Marcus, I do, but every week she's been calling later and later. I shelve the book for school and check out the other one. Katie calls as I'm heading to the car.

"Finally," I tell her. "Meet you at the rec center?"

"Can you pick me up at eleven?"

"Eleven? What am I supposed to do after the mall closes, sit in the parking lot?"

"Sorry," she says. "I just . . . I don't want to go home yet."

Normally I wouldn't even really hear that—she says it every time—but tonight I do because I think about her face when she was talking about her mom, about her brothers. "Katie . . ."

"Hold on . . ." I hear rustling and Marcus's voice mumbling, and then Katie says, "Can I say I spent the night at your house?"

I think for a second. Odds of Katie's mom calling my house to see if she's there—pretty low. Odds of Marcus's mom calling—higher, especially since there won't be an answer at Katie's, but the phone in Dad's room hasn't worked since I dropped it eight months ago, and he hasn't noticed yet. Plus I could turn the volume on the answering machine way down so he'd never hear if it clicked on. And Marcus's mom is probably far more likely to call whoever he's supposed to be with anyway. "Sure."

"Thank you." Katie's voice is practically a song, she sounds so happy. "I have to go home in the morning to make sure Harold and Gerald get to school okay, so I'll pick you up regular time?"

"You're going to spend the night with Marcus in his car and then go home at four in the morning or something? Are you sure you don't want to just go home now?" I mean, I get that she loves Marcus, but this much?

"The birthday party is tomorrow," she says, and then lowers her voice. "I'm—I feel like my whole life is taking care of them. I need some time to be . . . to be me. I promise I won't ask for anything like this again."

"It's not that. I just—Are you sure you want to go to school tomorrow? I mean, I could get Dad to drop me off. Or something. And then you could relax and get ready for the party, just hang out at home and—"

"I'd rather be at school. I'll see you tomorrow, okay?"

"Okay," I tell her, and we say good-bye. I wonder what Marcus will do after dropping off Katie, or who he's going to claim to be with, but that's not my problem. That is one good thing about dating Dave. Nothing like this would ever happen between us. What we have is totally straightforward, uncomplicated. Safe.

There's no way Dad will be home before ten thirty at the earliest, so I drive around for a while. I pass the high school, boring-looking even in the dark, and the mall, which tries (and fails) to compete with the big one in Broad Falls. I even drive past the few office buildings in Hamilton's so-called business district, tiny brick buildings nestled together, most of which have FOR SALE OR RENT signs flapping near them, and then past the entrance for Anderson Freight. It's all lit up, and I can hear the sounds of trucks driving in, see a line of them sitting by the side of the road, waiting to pass through the gate.

After I pass Anderson there isn't much to see. Aside from the Gas 'n' Go, which is the only place in town to buy a decent slushee, the road I'm on wanders past all the closed factories before heading to the highway. I don't feel the need to see any of that, so I decide to stop, buy myself a drink, and then head home.

The clerk glances up when I walk in, and then goes back to looking bored. The only other person in the store is standing in the middle of an aisle, staring at a shelf, and as I get closer I realize it's Evan. He doesn't even look up as I walk by, just keeps staring at the shelf. His eyes are almost closed, like he's falling asleep. I watch him while I get a slushee. He's just standing there, but now he's staring at the floor. I walk toward the counter. He's still there. I clear my throat. Nothing. The clerk is giving me the please-pay-for-your-purchase-and-get-out look. I ignore her and turn around, head toward him.

"Hey."

He doesn't say anything. He doesn't even look at me, just stands there with his hands in his pockets, his gaze focused on the floor.

"Evan?"

"Lauren?" he says slowly, his voice faint, hoarse. He looks at me then, really looks at me, and it's like he's never seen me before. His eyes are huge and look kind of out of it.

"Are you okay?"

"I'm fine," he says. And then he brushes past me, heading toward the front of the store. I turn around and watch him, wanting to do something, to say something, but not knowing what. He nudges open the door with his shoulder and then he's gone, swallowed up by the darkness of the parking lot. I look at what Evan was staring at—gauze pads and baby food—and the clerk fake coughs. I look over, catch her glare, and go pay for my slushee.

I head outside after I'm given my thirteen cents change, digging around in my pocket for the keys with one hand while my slushee freezes off the fingers of my other. At the far end of the parking lot, past the well-lit gas pumps and over in the dark by the car wash that, as far as I know, has never worked, someone is leaning against a car. Evan's car.

I walk toward it. He straightens up as I get closer, starts to open his door. "Sorry about before," he says. His voice still sounds strange. "I'm just—I didn't expect to see you."

I start to babble something stupid about slushees when the streetlight above the car wash flickers and I can see him clearly for a moment. Something has happened to his right hand. He's got it curled up in a loose fist resting on his window, but even so I can see it's swollen, the skin mottled dark with bruises.

"What happened?" I fumble with the cup I'm holding, pop open the lid. "Do you want some ice? It's slushee ice, but still." I hold it out to him.

He doesn't take it. "I'm fine," he says tightly.

"But your hand—"

"It's not that bad."

"Shouldn't you go to the emergency room?"

"No," he says sharply. "I'm just going to drive home and put some ice on it."

"Hello." I wave the cup at him. He makes a grimace that I think is supposed to be a smile and starts to get in his car.

"Really, I'm okay."

"I could drive you home."

He pauses, then shakes his head. "I can't leave the car here."

"If you called your mom maybe she could come and—"

"No." He says it really fast, almost panicked.

"Then at least let me follow you home." I can't believe I just said that. "I mean, to make sure you get there okay." I hope my face isn't as red as it feels.

"Are you sure you want to do that? I mean, you probably want to go home, talk to Dave—" The name just sort of hangs there in the air between us. Dave. My boyfriend.

"He, uh—" I almost say "he wouldn't mind" and the truth is, Dave would probably insist on driving Evan home himself—he's that kind of guy—but what comes out is, "He isn't home. And, you know, I still owe you for that time I crashed my bike into the bushes."

"Bushes?" And then Evan smiles. It lights up his face, makes my breath catch. "Oh yeah. I guess you do owe me. But you don't have to do this. I mean, I'm fine, really, and—"

"I want to," I say, and we both sort of stare at each other for a moment.

"Okay," he finally says softly, and gets in his car. "It's not that far away anyway."

"Okay," I echo back and head to my car.

Evan lives in one of the apartment complexes out past the new strip mall. There are four of them, and he lives in the third one. It looks like all the others, beige and bland with every apartment offering the exact same balcony, the exact same view of other balconies around it. He lives in the back of the complex, and when we get there he parks, walks over to my car, and taps on my window. When I roll it down he says, "Thanks."

"Evan," I say, and his name sounds both unfamiliar and familiar on my tongue, the sound of it making something race inside me. This time I'm not going to turn away without speaking. "Let me help you."

He's silent for a moment, a long moment, but then says, "Park over there," and points at a parking space. It's almost eerily quiet when I get out of the car. The way my dad talks about the apartment complexes—he hates them, says they drive property values down—you'd think they were falling apart and always noisy. But they aren't. They may look the same, but I've seen enough of Dad's houses to know that even the fanciest homes are the same under the surface. You have your bathrooms, your bedrooms, your kitchen, your dining room. Space only adds so much, usually rooms that aren't ever used, and if Dad and I lived in one of these apartments it would be filled with silence just like at home.

Evan lives on the third floor, and when we reach his door he fumbles with his keys. Under the glow of the walkway lights, he's so pale he looks almost inhuman. I reach over and take the keys out of his hand, my skin prickling as our fingers touch. I wonder if he notices and know he does. I can feel it, the air around us somehow becoming quieter, closer.

I thumb through his keys till I find one that looks like an apartment key and slide it into the lock. I turn it the wrong way at first, but eventually I hear a click and push the door open. There's a light on in the back, another one in the kitchen.

"Is your mom—?" I gesture inside, wonder what Mary will say when she sees me, if she will recognize me.

"She's at work. That's why I can't go to the emergency room and couldn't call her about the car. If I did any of that, she'd totally freak out. She knows I have a job, but I sort of lied about how many hours I was working and didn't—I didn't tell her exactly where it was. If she knew all of it, she'd . . ." He trails off.

"But your hand—" I say and reach out, take it gently in mine. It looks awful. He's hurt, and my heart shouldn't be racing like this but it is. It is.

"It looks worse than it is. I just need to put some ice on it, take some aspirin." He is looking down at his hand, at my hand holding his. He moves his fingers a little, brushing them across one of my palms. "Thank you for making sure I got home okay."

"At least let me get you the ice and aspirin."

"Lauren—" The way he says my name makes my breath catch.

"Tell me where," I say, and I hardly recognize my voice as my own.

The apartment is tiny, and Evan is right there, behind me, next to me. All I can think about. We stand in the kitchen—which looks comfortable, lived-in, a jar of peanut butter and a half-empty bottle of aspirin sitting on the counter—and I fumble with the ice trays in the freezer, popping cubes out and putting them in a towel, and then placing it gently on Evan's hand. He is looking at me, and I am looking back at him, and it feels like there is no air in this room, in the whole world. It feels like there's nothing but us, and part of me wants to leave, is desperate to, doesn't like how I'm feeling.

I don't leave. I grab the aspirin next, open the bottle, and pass Evan three. I watch him open a cabinet, and I stare at his back, at the line of his shoulders, the way his shirt rises in the back to show just a hint of skin. I've heard Katie talk about Marcus's arms and eyes like they were poetry, nodded, and looked at Dave as if I understood. I didn't, but I do now.

Evan has turned around, glass in hand, and for a moment the way his arm is extended makes me think that he's trying to get me to move closer, that he wants to pull me into his arms. But then the light overhead flickers, and I see the way he's trying to balance the ice on his other hand and realize he needs help. I'm standing here thinking—things—and he's in pain.

"Sorry," I say, and take the glass out of his hand, fill it with water, and hand it back to him. "I was just—" I make a floating motion with my hand, as if my thoughts had gone someplace else, away from him.

He puts the glass in the sink, leaning toward me, and I try not to notice him standing next to me. I try not to listen to him breathe, not to see him out of the corner of my eye, not to notice the way his hair has fallen into his eyes again, like it's just waiting for me to reach up and touch it, push it away, and look into his eyes.

"I should go," I say, turning toward him, and at the same time he turns toward me and says, "It's pretty late," and then we are both standing there, right next to each other. Looking at each other, so close. I can't hear anything but my heart racing, pounding inside my chest like it's trying to break free.

He kisses me. I know it's coming in a way I've never known anything, everything inside me suspended, waiting, and at the first brush of his mouth against mine I feel something inside me breaking open, spilling out everywhere. I have been kissed before, have waited to be kissed before, but not like this, never like this. Before I could always think, "Oh, here I am, kissing." I could see myself in the moment. But now I am unable to think anything but scattered, fleeting thoughts; that he tastes like water, that his hair is soft under my fingers, that even when we are closer, pressed together, it's not enough. I have never felt like this before.

His hand is on my waist, and my hand is on his back,

sliding down the line of his spine, over the skin that lies bare and warm where his shirt has ridden up. I taste aspirin bitter on his tongue, and I am drowning. We have turned, moving together, and I am pressed back against a counter, head thrown back. I'm surrounded by him. His hand is still on my waist, and I want it to move higher, I want it to move lower. Ice cracks in the towel, leaking cold water onto his hand, onto me, and I want. I want him.

He is saying something, his mouth shaping letters against mine, into me, and then he is pulling away, trembling against me. "Lauren," he says, and his voice is shaking, stunned.

In the microwave behind him, across from us, I see a reflection of myself. I do not recognize me. There is a wildness in my face, in my eyes, that I have never seen. That I have always feared.

I look at him, and he looks like how I feel, his eyes hot, his expression startled, shaken. He takes a step back, and we are staring at each other. It would take nothing to close the distance between us.

I want it closed. He is standing there silent and bruised, and I have been reckless, I have been worse than reckless, and I want it all and more again.

I have to get out of here.

I want to say that I hear myself say something, even "I have to go," in some stupid wobbly bad television movie voice. But the truth is I don't say anything. I just push past him and I run. Out of the kitchen, out of the apartment, down the stairs, and to the car. I don't look back.

fifteen

When I get home Dad is there. I throw my melted slushee in the garage trash can, my hands shaking, and walk into the house. He is waiting for me, sitting at the kitchen table, drumming the fingers of one hand against its surface, not even talking on his cell phone. He looks tired and angry and maybe even a little scared.

"Lauren," he says. My father does not yell at me, ever. I sometimes wish he did because then I would know what to do, could yell back and perhaps run upstairs and into my room, slam the door closed behind me. But when my father is angry with me he is quiet, his voice like a whip, a sharp crack of sound, but never louder than normal conversation. He yells at work, about work, and I've heard that. He and Mom yelled, and all the women who have lived here since have definitely had arguments with him, heard him be sarcastic or bitter or both and always loud. But he's never been any of that with me. Not once. And it isn't that I'm not used to this; to how he is with me, but my eyes suddenly fill with tears. I can't do this now. I am exhausted, overwhelmed by myself and this night. I'm scared.

I think maybe he sees that because his fingers stop tapping and his face shifts again, the anger falling away altogether. "Are you all right?"

I nod because if I talk, I will cry, and I do not want that. I hate crying, can deal with feeling the need to but not with it actually happening. I know I should say something, anything, but in my head I am still back at Evan's, and what happened is happening over and over again, and I can't see past it. I wish, suddenly and desperately, for my mother. No, not for her, but for what I wish she could have been, someone who would look at me and see that something has happened, fold me into her arms and just hold me, tell me that everything will be fine. I do not wish for my mother with her faraway eyes filled with an expression I have recently seen in my own.

Dad clears his throat and stands up, his chair scraping awkwardly across the floor. "You should have asked for permission to take the car," he says, and he doesn't sound angry at all. He sounds like he has no idea what to say, and when I blink hard, willing my eyes to stop burning, he glances away from me as if he doesn't want to see me like this. I suppose he probably doesn't, that maybe Mom stood across from him with her eyes looking just like mine, wild and upset.

"I'm sorry," I manage to squeeze out, my voice trembling. "I left you a message telling you about it."

"Oh," he says, and normally this is where I would tease him, laugh about his inability to listen to a message all the way through, careful to keep any hurt from my eyes, my voice. I would make everything okay. I shift my weight from one foot to another instead, silent, and he moves toward me. Just a little, a hesitant step around his chair, and for a crazy second I think that maybe he is going to try, that he will ask me a real question or even tell me everything will be all right, but instead he stops, sits back down, and just says, "I was worried."

"I'm sorry," I say again, and head out of the kitchen toward the stairs, toward my room. I see him as I am walking upstairs, still sitting at the table, staring down at it like it is the most fascinating thing he's ever seen. I should go back and offer to make him a sandwich, smile and smooth things over.

My hands are shaking on the bannister and I can't. I am raw inside, scared, and I don't know how to make things right or to even pretend to feel that way.

I wash my face and brush my teeth and change into pajamas, and then sit on my bed. It was just a kiss, I tell myself. Just a kiss. Not a big deal.

I can't sleep. I try, turn the lights out and slide under the covers, but I just lie there with my eyes wide open. I hear Dad downstairs moving around, hear him go into his study and shut the door. I get out of bed and go over to my computer, turn it on.

It was just a kiss, but how I felt during it was startling. Overwhelming. New.

I sign on to my instant message account. Katie isn't online, of course, and I wonder what she would say if I told her what happened. She would be angry, I think. Dave is Marcus's friend, and she would remind me of that. She would remind me how Dave arranged for Marcus and Katie to come out with us one night, how he smiled after they got together and said he knew they'd be perfect for each other. She would remind me that Dave is who I should have been thinking about. Who I should be thinking about.

Dave, who is online now and probably typing a message to me.

I click through the settings and pull up the block list, type Dave's name into it. Instantly he vanishes from sight, his name dropping off my friends list, and I know I have disappeared off his. I look at the other names on my list. There's no one I want to talk to. No one I really even know. Everyone besides Katie is Dave's friend, people who sometimes message me to ask what he's doing on the weekend when they can't reach him. I definitely can't talk to them.

I wonder what Evan's screen name is. I wonder if he is online now. I think about his body pressed against mine, his mouth forming my name.

I don't know what to do. I don't know how to feel about how I feel. I need to talk to someone. It's been a long time since I've felt this way, but I do now. All of this, everything that's happened—it's too huge to keep inside. And I think maybe I know someone who will listen. Maybe even understand. I grab the student directory and look up Gail's e-mail address. I type it into the little search box, and her user name pops up. She's online.

I click on her user name and type, "Hey."

After a pause the little window flashes, signaling a reply.

"Hey."

I bite my lip and type.

I can't bring myself to tell Gail everything, or anything, really—every time I try to, it's like my mind freezes up and I can't think of how to say what I want to—but she must be able to tell I'm upset because after a few minutes of conversation that run along the lines of her asking me how I felt about the concert and me saying, "What?" she asks if I want to meet for breakfast. I say yes and we make plans, and then I sign off and go back to bed.

I think I won't sleep, but I do. I don't remember having any dreams, but the first thing I think about when I wake up is last night and Evan. I hear Dad up and moving around, getting ready to leave, and I take the world's quickest shower, throw on some clothes, and race downstairs. I ask him if he can take me over to the diner by the community college. I can tell he wants to ask why, and I even sort of want him to ask, but he doesn't, just says, "Don't forget your bag."

"Thanks," I say, and grab it, realize it's full of homework I was supposed to do last night.

On the way to the diner Dad listens to classical music and talks on his phone. I look out the window and try to think about what I will do in my classes if I am called on.

I think about Evan instead. I wonder what will happen

when I see him. I know what I want to happen, I think, and rub my hands across my jeans, curling my fingers into the fabric behind my knees.

When Dad drops me off, he puts whoever he is talking to on hold and turns to me. He clears his throat once, twice, and then passes me a twenty. "For breakfast."

"Thanks," I tell him, and get out of the car.

As I'm shutting the door he says, "Lee Lee, you know I . . . Have a good day, okay?"

"I will," I say, and shut the door. I watch him drive away, my eyes stinging a little again. Twice in less than a day, and right now I'm confused and scared, and I can't keep it inside. I don't want to. It's a new feeling, a strange one, and part of me wants to pretend it all away, turn around and go.

But I don't.

Gail's in a booth in the back, and she waves when I come in. As I sit down, I notice she is looking at me strangely.

"Sorry," I tell her. "I didn't have time to put on makeup so I'm a total mess. And I know my hair—"

"Your shirt's on inside out," she says, her mouth twitching at the corners, and I look down and sure enough it is. And backward to boot. I laugh and Gail laughs too, and it's then I know that this—talking to her last night and now coming here—is the right thing to do. And before I know it, I've told her everything, words pouring out of me like they haven't . . . well, ever. I pause only long enough for the waitress to take our order, and then again when she brings us our coffee.

"And then I came home and my dad was waiting for me, and I knew he could tell something was wrong but he didn't know what to do and I didn't know what to do, and so . . ." I trail off.

"So your dad and his mom—?"

"Lived together for a few months when we were little. That's how we met. And then they split up."

"And you haven't seen him since?"

"Nope. Not until term started. And I know it wasn't that long ago, but it feels like—I feel like everything has changed."

"Because of last night?"

I nod. "But before that too. I just—" I bite my lip and look down at the table, then at Gail. She doesn't look angry or uncomfortable. She just looks like she wants to hear what I have to say. "I haven't been able to stop thinking about him since I saw him in world history."

Gail pours cream into her coffee and then takes a sip. "I wondered what was going on."

"What do you mean?"

"You're always staring at each other."

I flush, feel a wave of heat sweep up over my face. "We are?"

She nods. "And so this"— she points at my shirt, grinning— "is because of last night? That must have been some kiss."

I nod and take a sip of coffee. "It was. I mean, I know it was just a kiss, but—"

"Hey, some kisses are special. Some kisses—" Gail circles her hands in the air. "It's like they open a whole world."

That's exactly it. Exactly how I felt. When I tell her that, she looks pointedly at my shirt again and we both giggle.

"But it was—I've never felt like that," I tell her. "I'm not sure I want to feel like that."

The waitress arrives with our breakfast, and Gail and I eat, silent for the moment. As I'm finishing my eggs she says, "I get that. It's like there are people you can like and control how much you like them, right? But then there are other people, people who when you're with them you can't—you can't make yourself safe. And it feels great but it's also kind of—"

"Scary."

Gail pushes a toast crust around her plate. "Yeah. I felt like that when I met Jennie."

"Jennie?"

"My girlfriend," Gail says, and now I get what Carl was saying on the bus ride to the concert. I look at her, and she is looking back at me, wariness in her eyes. "I met her and suddenly I was overwhelmed with . . . well, everything. Every time I was around her it was like I couldn't think past her. I'd never felt like that before and it felt really great and really fucking scary at the same time."

"And now?"

Gail smiles, the wariness in her eyes fading. "It's still scary sometimes. But mostly it's just really great. It's just you have to—I don't know. Let go of being scared or something. Just be who you are."

But what if who I am is like my mother? If I felt like I did last night all the time—I take another sip of coffee. "But what if who I am isn't . . . what if I'm better off now? I'm still me and

I'm never—" I point at my shirt. "I'm never like this."

"I don't know," Gail says. "But when you talk about him—Lauren, I've only ever seen you look like that the day you got the solo."

I think of how my face looked that day, how I thought I'd never seen myself look so happy. I think about my mother with her shining eyes that looked first at my father and then at me. I think about how it all changed, everything she felt fading until the only thing she wanted was to be gone. I don't want to lose myself like that. I don't want to be like that.

"Enough about me," I tell her. "You have any pictures of you and Jennie?"

Gail and I end up talking for a long time. I look at pictures of her and Jennie, and we talk about how they met. Gail smiles every time she says Jennie's name. We talk about music and our other classes. We talk about books, about movies. About everything. Katie texts me once, when I'm in the bathroom turning my shirt right side out and around the right way, wanting to know where I am and if I'm okay. I quickly text back that I'm fine and we'll talk later, and then turn my phone off.

Gail and I talk for so long that we have to race out of the diner and to her car, speed all the way to school. And even then we're still late for our first classes. But it was worth it, and I tell her that as we're walking in. "This was totally worth the tardy I'm going to get."

"I've never gotten one before," she tells me, and then adds, smiling, "but it really was worth it."

sixteen

As soon as I get to lunch, Katie pulls me aside.

"Where were you this morning?"

"Just—you know. I went to grab some breakfast."

"You should have called me."

"Sorry," I mumble. "You want to get a soda? I hear they finally got something besides diet ginger ale."

"Lauren. I went by your house and you weren't there. I knocked on the door for, like, ten minutes and then thought—God, I thought something had happened to you, and I didn't know what to do—" She breaks off and glares at me, her mouth trembling a little like it does when she's really upset and trying not to cry.

Shit. "Sorry," I say again. "Didn't you get my text message?"

She stares at me. "You mean your reply to the one I sent asking where you were and what was going on? The one where you said, 'Am fine talk later'? Yeah, I got it." She shakes her head. "I can't believe you. I'd never do something like that to you."

"Well, some of us aren't as perfect as you are."

She turns around and walks off, heading toward the line for pizza. I chase after her, touch her arm.

"Katie—"

"Sometimes I think you don't like me at all, Lauren. And you're my best friend. What kind of person am I if my best friend hates me?" Her lower lip trembles again.

"I don't hate you. I suck, okay? Something came up at the last minute, but I should have called. It was really shitty of me. I won't ever do it again, I promise."

"It's not just that. It's—you've been different lately. And we don't ever talk about anything."

"Hey, didn't I just tell you they finally got some decent soda in?"

She rolls her eyes at me but smiles a little. "You know you can tell me anything."

No, I can't. But I don't say that. I just say, "I know," and wait in line with her, buy her a piece of pizza, and ask about her and Marcus.

It turns out things didn't really work out. It got a lot colder in the car than they thought it would ("not romantic cold, just cold cold"), and some cops came around and tapped on the window, threatened to call their parents. "And his mom," she says. "I swear, it was like she knew because she kept calling every five minutes. Did he need a toothbrush? 'Cause she could bring one right over. Did he need his contact lens case? 'Cause she noticed he'd left it. And then she called and said something about his dad getting hurt at work and how she had to go get him, and he ended up having to take me home way early."

"That sucks. Is his dad all right?"

"Yeah," she says. "Marcus says he's going to be fine. Look at Dave waving. It's so cute how he is around you. And look"—she points at a table—"all those freshman girls are practically melting in envy."

I look, and sure enough, the girls are gazing at Dave and then at me like we're something amazing. "They probably can't figure out why he's dating me."

"Are you kidding? They want to be you. You're so lucky."

We reach the table, and I watch her lean down and kiss Marcus, watch him wrap his arms around her like he doesn't ever want to let her go. "That's me," I say, and sit down, leaning over a bit so Dave can press a quick kiss to my cheek.

Katie unwinds herself from Marcus and looks at me. I grin at her, fast and wide, and then turn away to talk to Dave. We both say we're sorry we didn't get to see each other this morning, and he apologizes for not calling last night. "John's practice ran really late, and then I took him to the mall to get something to eat."

"You must have just missed each other," Katie says. "Lauren was at the mall last night too."

I nod and Katie is still looking at me, head tilted a little to one side. "Yep," I say brightly, and lean over to rest my head against Dave's shoulder, the happy couple pose. "I wish I'd seen you."

"I guess it was a night of misses. I thought I saw you online later, but you vanished before I could send you a message. Lots of homework?"

"Too much," I say, and lean over to snatch Katie's pizza crust, not looking at her at all.

As I'm eating it, I think about how much I hate lunch. For one thing, I don't fit in here, at this table. All of the people I sit with, except for Katie, are Dave's friends, the popular crowd that worships him and tolerates me because I'm with him. And on days when Dave isn't here I—well, I eat lunch outside, on the far side of the school. I know how it sounds, but I also know what would happen if I went to that table by myself, and it wouldn't be pretty. I'd probably be allowed to sit, and Katie and Marcus would talk to me, but I'd be discussed by everyone else and found wanting. There would be enough whispers and pointed looks so I'd know it, but that would be all and if I tried to tell Dave about it, I wouldn't have anything specific to say.

Not that I would tell Dave, even if I were stupid enough to try to sit at the table when he isn't here. Dave and I just don't talk about stuff like that. I mean, we do talk, but I'm always careful to be the girl he loves, the Lauren I wish I could be, who is a lot more perfect than I am.

"Does it sound okay?" he says, and I blink, look at him, and am stunned yet again by how cute he is. And by how I have no idea what he's talking about.

"Does what sound okay?"

"My new training schedule," he says, grinning. "What do you think?"

I think that last night I was kissing Evan Kirkland. I wonder what he thinks about it. I wonder what he's doing now. I'm going to see him in a few hours and—Oh God, I'm going to see him. I ran out of his apartment like a total drama queen and was so caught up in thinking about the kiss I didn't think about anything else. What am I going to do when I see him?

"Seriously," Dave says, sliding his arms around me and pulling me close. "What do you think?"

I want to kiss Evan again.

I barely manage to get through the rest of lunch, nod and smile at Dave while I sit there, unable to stop thinking about Evan. After music, Gail and I duck into the bathroom and talk really fast about the whole thing, and it's nice to have an actual conversation and not just Katie shoving mints at me, although the minute we walk into Axel's class I wish I'd had some because Evan is there, sitting slouched in his desk and shoving his hair out of his eyes to look at me.

"Is there a reason you can't take your seat, Miss Smith?" Axel asks, and I shake my head, feel my face heat up. I sit down, look over at Gail. She's bent over her notebook but glances up and mouths, "He's staring," at me.

I dare another quick glance at Evan as I sit down, and he is looking at me, a little half smile on his face. And when he sees I'm looking at him his smile stretches, leaps up into his eyes. I smile back. Axel drones on, something about a battle or a castle or maybe both, and taps the textbook the way she does when she's telling us something that's going to be on a test. I look at Evan's hand. It looks both better and worse today, less swollen, but the bruises are darker, a deep blue-purple. I scratch, "Are you okay?" across my notebook and turn it so he can see it.

I wait for him to write something down in his own notebook or to shrug or—I don't know, really—but instead he is leaning across his desk and over onto mine. His pen marches across my notebook, and his hair brushes against my cheek for a second before he's gone, back in his own seat. I look down at my notebook.

"Better. Will you meet me in the library after school?"

I look over at him and nod. Yes. Yes, I will. I should meet Katie and walk out of school with her, get a hug and a kiss and a promise of a phone call or message later from Dave.

Should, but I'm not going to.

When the bell finally rings—I swear the clock was moving backward at one point—Axel stops droning and everyone races out into the hall. Evan looks over his shoulder as he goes, giving me a quick smile, and I smile back, then get out my phone and send Katie a text telling her I don't need a ride home. Gail walks by as I'm finishing and I mouth, "Talk later?" She nods, and I finally get why Katie tells me every single way-too-much-information detail about her and Marcus. Talking about someone who makes you happy actually makes you happy. Being happy makes you want to talk, to go over everything, to share it so you can remember it all over again. No wonder my GPA isn't all that great. Seventeen and I'm just now realizing this?

When I get to the library, Evan is there, talking to the librarian. She's actually smiling at him, and as I walk up to them, she even laughs.

"Okay, what did you do to her?" I ask as we're sitting down. "The last time I was in here all she did was glare."

"I've just got a way with the ladies."

I laugh and Evan makes a mock-offended face and says, "What? Just because you fled in terror doesn't mean—"

"It wasn't terror."

"You sure?" His voice is teasing, but there is seriousness in there too.

I nod, and his uninjured hand moves across the table, fingers brushing against mine.

"I like you," he says. Just like that. Like it can just be that easy.

I stare at him, my insides totally turned to mush by what he's said, by his smile, by how his eyes crinkle at the corners and his hair flops into his eyes. I'm totally unsettled and completely happy around him, and it scares me.

"I like you too," I say, linking my fingers through his, and the scariest thing of all is that when I'm with him, everything does seem like maybe it can be that easy.

We stay in the library till just after four, when the librarian tells us she has to go to a meeting.

"You want a ride home?" he asks, and I nod. The smile on my face feels like sunshine.

On the way to the car he asks about music, and before I know it I am telling him about the concert and my solo and how it felt. As we drive he tells me about the first time he ever played in front of anyone. "A crowd of three college kids. Three drunk college kids, even. I still felt like I was going to vomit in terror anyway."

"And did you?"

"Nope." He grins at me. "Walked out onstage, thought I was going to for sure. Got behind the keyboards and felt great. Started playing, went to pull the mic up a bit and"—he mimes it smacking him in the head—"spent the next couple of days wishing I'd just thrown up."

I laugh, and then realize we are turning down the road to my house.

"You should come in," I tell him. "I mean, if you want to." Oh my God, shut up, Lauren. "Do you want to?" I force my mouth closed.

He looks over at me, then back at the road. His smile has faded a little.

"Okay," he says, and this time he does not stop at the end of my driveway. He drives all the way up to the house, and then we sit there, in silence, looking at it.

"Is that big tree still in the backyard?" he finally says.

"No. Dad put a pool in, and all the trees got taken out. We planted more, but they've never really grown. Dad says it's because—" I break off, embarrassed by the way I'm babbling again.

"I never wanted to see this place again," he says quietly, and that thing people say about their heart sinking? It's actually true. I feel it happening to me, this horrible dropping pain inside me. Everything was so great and now I've totally ruined it. I don't know why this surprises me, but it does and it hurts. It hurts a lot.

"Sorry," I mutter, and reach for the door.

"Don't be," he says, and touches my arm. "I didn't—that came out all wrong. I thought I'd never want to see it again but now that I have it's—it's just a house. Your house. And so—"

"So?" My heart is pounding so hard I can hardly hear myself talk.

He grins at me. "So do I get to see it, or should I stay out here and you can—I don't know, go inside and open windows and hang things out for me to see?"

I grin back at him, flooded with happiness, and he's close enough for me to lean over and press my mouth to his. So I do. Because I want to. Because I'm really starting to believe that with him, it can be that easy.

Inside the house it's quiet just like always. He whistles at the kitchen. "Oh yeah," I say. "Robin, the last girlfriend—she liked to cook."

"It's nice," he says, and points at the fridge. "Is that made of wood?"

"It's supposed to look like it," I tell him. It matches the cabinets. Our whole house is a showcase for Dad's design ideas, which means he's forever putting in new windows or having various rooms repainted or totally redecorated. So far my room has been safe, but I'm sure the first time I come home from college it will look completely different. I pull the fridge open, and we stand there, looking at the mostly empty shelves.

"Now that looks like mine," he says. I look over at him, and he's leaning toward me and I am leaning toward him and—

"Lee Lee?"

Dad? It can't be, but at the sound of another voice both Evan and I step back, away from each other, and I smack my head on the part of the fridge door that's supposed to hold eggs.

"Lee Lee, did you just hit your head?"

It is Dad. Never home, except for today. Figures. "Hi," I say to him and shut the fridge door, conscious of Evan standing very still and very silent beside me. "What are you doing home?"

"Videoconferencing thing. The connection at work died and so—oh." He looks at Evan, then back at me. "I thought I heard a car but wasn't sure—I didn't realize you had company."

I wait for him to say something else. To actually notice who I am with.

"Yeah," I say, when he just keeps standing there looking at me, "Evan brought me home."

"Ah," Dad says, and looks at Evan again. "Hi there, nice to meet you. I'm—"

"I know who you are," Evan says, and his voice is suddenly icy cold, harsh.

"Dad," I say desperately. "It's Evan."

"Well, Evan, she must really like you since she's giving me

a please-don't-say-anything-stupid look," Dad says, trying some bizarre charming routine, and I could kill him.

"Mary," I tell him. "Dad, he's Mary's son."

"Mary?" Next to me, I hear Evan suck in a breath.

Oh God, Dad, no. Come on.

"Oh," Dad says, finally remembering, but it's too late and he knows it because his voice has gone from jaunty into fake jaunty. "How's she doing?"

"Fine," Evan says. "I have to go."

And just like that he's gone, out of the house and into his car. I see him back down the driveway, hear the squeal of tires as he pulls away onto the road.

"Well," Dad says, "it's nice to know he's doing so well."

I stare at him, thinking, Were you here for the same conversation I was? Did you hear how he reacted when you didn't remember him? When you didn't remember his mother? "You'd better get back to your videoconference."

"It's been a long time, Lauren. He was just a kid when—"

"So if I'd been her daughter, you would have forgotten me?"

"Lee Lee—"

"Don't call me that," I say, and open the fridge again, stare inside till I hear him walk away.

seventeen

Gail's advice, when I tell her everything that night over instant message, is short and to the point: "Talk to him." I tell her she's right and that I will, and decide I'll tell Katie I have to do something for Mr. Herrity when we get to school in the morning so I can find Evan and talk to him. I had thought about driving out to Anderson Freight to see him, but Dad left to go back to the office as I was in the kitchen making dinner, and when I pointedly ignored his good-bye he stood there for a second before saying, "I'm sorry." I didn't expect that and probably would have forgiven him for earlier except that he took the other set of car keys when he went, like he knew what I was thinking about doing and didn't want me to do it. So I went back to being annoyed with him. Not that it mattered, as he wasn't home to see it.

Katie calls just as I'm telling Gail I'll talk to her tomorrow and am signing off.

"Why weren't you online this afternoon? I looked for you." Great, she's pissed again. I sprawl across my bed, cursing myself for not calling her earlier.

"Homework. And hey, I should have told you about having a ride home at lunch. I just totally forgot. God, I'm the worst friend ever."

I admit even I know the "No, you aren't" response isn't coming, but I'm still hurt when Katie says, "Yeah, lately you really have been. Who'd you get a ride with?"

I stay silent for a moment, hoping to hear Harold and Gerald screaming in the background so she'll say she has to go, but for once I guess they are behaving because there's nothing but quiet coming from her end of the line. "Evan," I finally say.

"Oh. Dave was looking for you, you know. Have you talked to him?"

"Yes." If a distracted twenty-minute phone call while I was eating dinner and staring at the fridge, thinking about Evan, counts.

"So pretty soon you guys will have been going out for, what, a year and a half?"

I so don't want to talk about Dave right now. "I gotta go," I tell her. "Dad just came home and is trying to make microwave popcorn. I have to make sure he doesn't burn the house down."

She doesn't laugh the way she normally would, just says, "Sure. I'll see you tomorrow morning. Right?" and hangs up before I can even reply. Shit.

When Katie comes to pick me up in the morning, I'm sitting outside waiting for her. "And," I say as I get in the car, "not only am I ready on time, I've even eaten. So no wrappers all over your car. This sort of makes up for yesterday, right?" Then I get a look at her. She looks like she always does, really, except for one thing. The nail polish on her right thumb is chipped, and so is the polish on her left pinky finger. Katie's nail polish is never chipped. Ever.

"What's going on?" I ask, and she looks over at me. She looks exhausted and like she's about to cry.

"Katie? Is it Marcus?"

She shakes her head. "The birthday party was last night. I wanted to have it on the weekend, but Harold and Gerald asked Dad about it when he was home, and he said having it on a school night was fine." She takes a deep breath. "When I called you last night, I was in a supply closet at the laser tag place, trying not to—" She breaks off, but she doesn't have to finish her sentence. Trying not to cry.

"Pull over," I tell her, and she does. I hug her, and she cries and tells me about the party. None of the other parents stayed so there she was, alone with twenty-five wound-up little kids, and by nine the laser tag people had asked her to leave twice. And by the time she finally did get everyone outside to wait for their parents, she and Harold and Gerald had been told they weren't welcome there again. Ever. "The manager kept asking where our parents were, kept saying, 'They can't be here for their kids' birthday?' You should have seen Harold's and Gerald's faces—"

"Oh no," I say, and I shouldn't be thinking about how I'm missing out on talking to Evan but I am, a little. I hug Katie again and tell her I'm sorry and wish I were a better person. Right now, even though all those books I read made me feel like shit, I'd kill to be like one of the girls in them, to be a perfect friend and not the kind who sits in a car on the side of the road listening to her best friend sob and feeling bad for her but also thinking about herself.

But I stay me, Miss So-Not-Perfect, and when we get to school just in time to haul ass to our first-period classes, I'm upset I didn't get a chance to talk to Evan, which makes me feel even worse about everything. I'm also worried because Katie, after telling me about the party, started asking about yesterday. She asked about yesterday a lot and in a way that means she knows something is going on, and not only do I not want to tell her anything, I don't want to even think about telling her anything.

Also, I still want to talk to Evan.

I don't get a chance to. I think about hanging around after lunch to see if I can run into him, but Dave surprises me by taking me out, coming up to me as I'm waiting in line with Katie for yet another exciting piece of pizza and whispering, "I have a surprise for you."

He takes me off campus, to the McDonald's out by the highway, and we sit in his car in the parking lot, talking about nothing. I'm eating fries, and Dave is eating the sandwich his mom made him, and the whole thing is—it doesn't feel like anything. Being with him doesn't feel like anything. It doesn't make me feel anything, and once we've made plans for the weekend (a church thing tonight, pizza with everyone and then a party on Saturday) and he runs out of sports stuff to talk about and I've asked about his parents there's nothing left to say; the drive back to school filled with silence. He seems fine with it. I look over at him as we're heading inside, and he is looking back at me, smiling.

"I'm glad we did this," he says. "Katie said you and I needed to spend some time together, and I think she's right. I haven't been around much lately, and I'm really sorry for that. I don't want you to think I'm taking you for granted or don't know how lucky I am."

"You're not that lucky," I mumble, but when Dave says, "What?" I just say, "Thanks for lunch," and watch people look at him as we walk down the hall.

The reality of that, of how everyone totally looks up to Dave, reminds me that I'm supposed to be the lucky one. He wants to be with me, and if I never feel overwhelmed with happiness when I'm with him, I'm also never sad, never worried. But still, as we're walking, his hand clasping mine, I realize that the way I'm feeling now would have felt fine a while ago. Maybe a little boring, but fine. But now it's not enough.

Now that I've felt more, I want to keep feeling that way. Even if it does scare me a little. Or a lot.

* * *

I'm a total disaster in music class. Gail and I pass notes back and forth the whole time, and I learn Gail and Jennie are going to go shopping for formal dresses this weekend because there's a big dance at Jennie's school—she goes to one of the high schools in Broad Falls—in a few weeks. I ask Gail what kind of dress she wants, and she answers but also writes, "Are you going to tell me what's going on with Evan or what?" Mr. Herrity sees me reading her note and clears his throat. I put it away and shrug at Gail.

Three seconds later my phone vibrates. She's sent me a text message asking the same thing she did in her note. So I raise my hand, ask to go to the bathroom, and when she comes in a few minutes later, I tell her everything. It's actually a total relief.

"Look," she says when I'm done talking. "When we get out of here, why don't you wait for him at the edge of the hall by Axel's class? Then when he walks by you can ask him if he wants to talk and skip class."

"You're suggesting I skip class? You?"

She rolls her eyes at me. "What did Axel talk about yesterday?"

"Um—battles. No, wait, castles. Both?"

"See? So just skip and talk to him already."

"Okay," I tell her, and we both head back to class. And then, as we're walking out afterward, heading toward Axel's class, Gail telling me about the dress Jennie is looking for and helping me keep an eye out for Evan, Katie appears.

"Hey," she says, and smiles at Gail briefly before tucking

her arm through mine and saying, "I've been dying to hear about your lunch!"

"Katie—"

"Hold on," she says, and digs through her purse with her other hand, coming up with the familiar tin of mints, which she passes to me. "So, tell me all about it. Did you and Dave have a good time?"

"Sure," I say around a mouthful of mints. She's walking me down the hallway, which won't work at all. I need to be waiting for Evan. "Look, you probably want to see Marcus before you go to class—"

"Come on, I want details."

And so I find myself telling her about lunch as she walks me all the way to Axel's class, lingering so I barely make it to my desk before the bell rings. No time to talk to Evan. And in class he doesn't look at me, or at least doesn't look at me when I look at him. I spend the whole period writing him notes, and then writing different ones because the ones I've written are all stupid. As Axel is winding her way down, lecturing us about whatever to the last possible second, I decide on a new plan. I'll wait around after class, see if Evan stays. If he does, I'll talk to him. If he doesn't . . . well, then I'll go to the library and talk to him.

The bell rings and everyone races for the door except me. I fiddle around in my seat for a second, pretending I can't find my pen, and then look over at Evan.

He's still there, and he's looking at me. This is it. Deep breath. I lean over and put my book in my bag, listen to the squeak of feet exiting the classroom. Okay. Now I'm just going to say I'm sorry about my father being an asshole and hopefully he'll say—

"Lauren, are you ready?"

Okay, that doesn't sound like Evan. That sounds like . . . "Katie?"

It is her. She's looking at me, a tense smile on her face. What is she doing here? I look around and Evan is still in the room, sliding his notebook into his bag. I wish she'd go away, and then I feel guilty. But I still say, "Hey, you don't need to wait for me. I'll catch up to you in just a minute."

"Sorry, but we have to leave right now. I've got to pick up my brothers, and besides, the sooner you get home, the sooner you can get ready to go out with Dave tonight. Oh! We need to talk about tomorrow too. I think we're all meeting up before going to someone's party."

Evan looks away from me, mouth twisted into this awful smirk-frown, and heads out of the room. I feel my face turn red, and I know he knows about Dave, but did Katie have to say it like that? Like so—I jam my book into my bag and stand up.

"Let's go," I say, and head out into the hallway without even waiting for her. I know I shouldn't be mad at her—Dave is the guy I'm going out with, and her talking about him isn't out of the ordinary—but I'm mad anyway.

On our way to the parking lot she starts to walk through the cafeteria, taking the long way that will lead us by the gym, and I know that means she wants to see Marcus.

"I thought we were in a hurry," I say.

She shrugs. "I thought you might want to see Dave."

"I don't want you to be late picking up Harold and Gerald."

"Oh, right," she says, sharp-edged, and an awkward silence falls between us as we turn back around and head straight to the parking lot. It doesn't end till we're in the car and she clears her throat and says, "So. Do you know who's having the party tomorrow?"

I shake my head. "You didn't have to come get me, you know. I was coming to find you."

Katie looks at me, and I can tell we both know I'm lying. After a second I look away, pretend I'm fascinated by what's going on out the window.

"Lauren," she says as we're turning down the road that leads to my subdivision, "is there something, you know . . . is there anything you want to talk about?"

I look over at her, at her perfect outfit and perfectly matching fingernails (of course she fixed her nail polish, of course she did), and wonder what she would say if I told her I was tired of perfection. I look at her and think of her and Marcus and how happy they are, and how Dave and I make them even more perfect because then we're all paired off, perfect matching sets, and know she wouldn't understand. She would say I have everything anyone could ever want, and she would be right. I have what—who—everyone wants.

But I want someone else.

eighteen

Dave and I spend Friday night at the church thing with his parents. I try really hard not to think about Evan during it. I am not successful. On Saturday I go grocery shopping and work on homework and talk to Katie, keep so busy I shouldn't have time to think about Evan. I do anyway. That night Dave picks me up in his mom's car, right on time as always. He actually seems sad that Dad, who is off taking care of some work crisis, isn't home. "I wanted to say hi," he says. "I feel like I haven't made a great impression."

Only Dave would take the fact that my father forgot who he was and turn it around so that he was the one who needed to do something. "You made a great impression."

"Really?"

I nod.

"Good." Dave smiles. "Because—well, this morning my parents said maybe the next time you come over for dinner you could bring your dad."

Oh yeah. I can't even get him to eat dinner with me. Plus, my dad in Dave's parents' house? I can just see it now. He'd chat away on his cell phone, and Dave's parents would be so nice about it, so understanding that I'd just want to crawl in a hole and die. "I'll ask him."

"Great." At the next stoplight Dave leans over and kisses me quickly. "I know I said something about Sunday afternoon last night, but it turns out I'm going with my parents to see John play in a skills challenge. He got invited because of how well he did in his last game."

"That's great." I wonder how much time Dave and I actually spend talking together, just the two of us, every week. I bet if you added it all up the conversation Evan and I had in the library a few days ago would be about six times longer.

Evan. I want to talk to him so badly.

Dave is still talking, telling me about what John will be doing, about how he'll be sure to call me afterward. I nod and wonder if Evan is at work tonight. I wonder if he's at home. If he's in his kitchen. I can see him there, watch him turn toward me, his head descending toward mine—

"Ready to go in?"

I blink. I'm in a car outside the pizza place. Dave's car. I'm with Dave. He asks if I'm okay, and I say I'm fine. He takes my hand and we head inside.

* * *

I think every single one of Dave's friends is here. Even Clara has made an appearance, sitting at the head of the table surrounded by her two current very best friends and getting constant phone calls. Apparently the mystery college boyfriend can't be here but sure does want to be. "He says he misses me," she says when she clicks her cell closed after the third call, rolling her eyes in a way that means she's acting annoyed but really wants us to wish we had college guys missing us. Katie laughs when I whisper that to her and stops looking quite so worried about the fact that Clara waved to Marcus when he and Katie sat down.

All the girls except Clara, who is taking yet another phone call, get up to go to the bathroom after the pizza is ordered. After a moment or two and a smiled "Don't worry, I'll order a soda for you," from Dave, I get up and follow them. I wish Katie was coming but know she won't because Clara waved at Marcus and Katie worries even though she doesn't need to.

In the bathroom, it's about what I expected. I stand around while everyone else talks, although one of the girls, Traci or Tami, does ask me if she can borrow a condom.

"Sure," I tell her, "but you don't really need to give it back," and fish through my purse as she looks at me blankly. I always have plenty of condoms. Katie buys buckets of them even though Marcus always has them too, and so she's always giving them to me so I can be "extra safe." For a while I would just throw them away, embarrassed by the fact that I was never going to need them, but then my natural laziness took over, and so now I have tons in my bag, along with about eighteen lipsticks and four combs.

The talk turns from "How's my hair?" to who is doing what and who they're doing it with, and I can't believe how boring it is. I see a couple of the girls look at me in the mirror and smile at them, trying even though I know it's pointless and I'm not even sure I want to. They nudge one another, so sure they know what keeps Dave with someone like me. I sigh and wish I were somewhere, anywhere else.

Actually that's not true. I wish I were—I let myself think about it as I head back to the table and sit down—I wish I were with Evan. I wish I were in his apartment, back when we were kissing. I wish we were in my house and that Dad wouldn't come in and wreck it all, that it would be just Evan and me and—

"We ordered a couple of pitchers of root beer," Dave says. "Is that okay? If you want water or something else, I can ask the waitress."

I have to talk to him.

"I need to go home," I say, and Dave blinks at me.

"What?"

"I feel really sick. Please just take me home."

"Of course," he says, worry in his voice and in his gorgeous eyes, and I'm lying.

I'm lying and he doesn't know it and I don't care. Katie catches my eye as we're getting up and Dave is explaining—not that anyone besides him and Katie and Marcus will even notice I'm gone—and I can tell she knows something is going on. I still don't care and when Dave and I walk out of the restaurant, I don't look back.

* * *

Dave walks me into the house, asks if I need a glass of water, some aspirin. He's been like that the whole way home, totally sweet and wonderful. It's driving me crazy.

"I just need to lie down," I tell him as I sit at the kitchen table, already wondering how long I should wait before I grab the car keys and head out to see if Evan is home, and am shocked to hear my father say, "Lee Lee, you're sick?"

I nod, too surprised to see him to actually say anything, and he looks at me for a second, then comes over and feels my forehead with the back of his hand. I don't think he's done that since I was a little kid.

"No fever," he says, and then turns to Dave and says, "Thanks for bringing her home."

"No problem, sir. And I want to apologize again for the other night. I should have called before I came over."

Dad looks at him blankly, and for a horrible second I think he's going to get Dave confused with Evan and mention the other day, but instead all he says is, "Not a problem."

"So I really should go lie down," I say, anxious to stop any further conversation. Anxious to have Dave leave, to have Dad wander back to doing whatever it is he's doing. Anxious to go find Evan.

"Of course," Dad says, and Dave gives me a quick kiss, promises to call me tomorrow, and tells me to feel better. He holds his hand out for my father to shake, and Dad does, tells him to drive safely. Once he's gone I wait for Dad to leave the room too, but he doesn't, just stands there looking at me.

"So," I finally say. "Guess you must have a lot of stuff to do."

He makes a vague agreeing noise and then says, "So, you and Dave . . . are things okay?"

"Dad."

"What? I can't ask?"

You don't care, I want to say, but just shrug instead. "Everything's fine."

Dad makes another vague noise. "I guess you'd better go lie down and rest."

"Actually, I'm feeling better and I . . . Well, I kind of—I need to borrow the car."

"Why?"

I look at him and he's looking at me, not in his usual distracted-by-the-phone way or even in his tired-from-a-long-day way, but actually looking at me. It's kind of strange.

But not strange enough to distract me. "I have to go somewhere."

"Where?"

I don't get what he's doing but that's okay. I know how to stop it. "Dad, if you have something to say, why don't you just say it?"

He opens his mouth, then closes it. No surprises there. I get up, grab the keys. "I'll be extra careful with the car, I promise."

"It's not the car I'm worried about," he says quietly.

I turn back toward him. "Dad—"

"Honey, I'm . . . I'm sorry I didn't remember Evan."

"Dad—"

"I saw the look on your face, Lauren. And I don't want you to think that I would ever—"

"I know," I say, suddenly sick of it all, of how there are so many things we don't ever talk about. That we pretend never happened. "You won't forget me. If nothing else, I have Mom's eyes, don't I? A reminder of someone who forgot you, every time you look at me."

He stares at me, a million expressions—shock, fury, sadness—flashing across his face. Now you know how I feel, I think, and slam the door when I leave.

I shouldn't have said that, I know. It was mean, and Mom is the biggest silence between us, that eats into the house, our lives. Into us. But I didn't want to hear what he had to say. I still can't believe he forgot someone he said was important to him, that he could see part of his past, part of his life, and not remember it at all.

It's not until I get to Evan's apartment that I get nervous. Well, more like move from very nervous to really very nervous. For a moment I sit in the car with my hands wrapped around the steering wheel. The engine is still on. I could just drive home. Dad will be in his study, probably on his phone or checking his e-mail, and more than likely wouldn't even come out to say good night. In the morning we won't mention any of this, and it will be like it never happened.

But I want to do this. I want to see Evan, talk to him. I

turn off the car and get out, walk up to his apartment. I knock on the door. Softly, just a brush of my knuckles, my nervousness suddenly returning worse than ever, but before I can do anything else the door opens and Evan is standing there.

He looks surprised to see me.

"Hey," I say, and he tilts his head to one side a bit, hair falling into his eyes, and says, "Hey," before motioning for me to come inside.

I walk in, see the kitchen just over to my right, a sofa and a television in the room in front of me. As the door closes we stand there for a moment, awkward, my mind apparently exhausted from the strain of saying hi, and then a gray cat appears from the hallway by the kitchen, winding around Evan's ankles and purring up at me before it saunters back down the hall.

"Yours?" Well, even though it's still only one word, at least it's a different one.

"Yeah," he says, and gives me one of those chewed-off smiles. "What's up?"

"I—I wanted to talk to you about my dad," I tell him, and his smile shrinks, goes bitter looking. Oh, this is bad. "Look, I'm sorry about the whole thing with him. He's . . . I was going to say you don't know how he is, but I guess you do."

"Yeah, I do. So you really didn't need to come by. I mean, especially since you have plans with Dave and everything." The way he says "Dave" makes my face flush.

"I don't—"

"What? Have a boyfriend?" Evan's smile is totally gone now. "Because I'm pretty sure you do. I thought, after we talked in the library that . . ." He shakes his head. "It doesn't matter. I heard your friend talking about you two after class on Friday. Hell, I saw you and him coming in after lunch holding hands, smiling. The perfect couple."

"We're not," I say. "God, we're so not. I mean, we're dating, but it's not—when I'm with him it's not like it is with you."

He gives me a look. I can't tell what it means.

"How's your hand?" I ask, desperate to get him to say something, to keep talking, but it's the wrong thing to say because I can definitely read his look now and it's nothing but anger.

"I got fired."

"Because you got hurt?"

He nods.

"But that's not fair. I mean, you got hurt at work so shouldn't they—?"

"What? Hold the job I'm not supposed to have until I'm better? Right. Not that I could go back even if there was a job. The second Mom saw my hand she freaked out, and now she calls to check up on me constantly, so even if I could get my job back there's no way I'd be able to keep it without her finding out."

"You know, my dad does tons of stuff with construction, and I'm sure he could find something—"

"I don't want anything from your father."

"Oh," I say stupidly, because of course he doesn't. After what happened when we were kids, and then with Dad not remembering him . . . God, after everything, I'm surprised he let me in tonight. I'm surprised he ever talked to me at all.

"I'm sorry," I tell him. "I'm so sorry about your hand and your job, and I shouldn't have come out here. I just—I wanted to see you and I couldn't—I had to see you, you know? I can't stop thinking about you."

Silence. I can't believe I said all that. I look at the floor, my eyes stinging.

"Lauren," he says, and when I look up at him he's staring at me, his eyes soft. He leans in, brushing my hair back from my face with his uninjured hand, and he smells wonderful, not like cologne but like soap and himself, this amazing scent. He's so close I can see his eyes are a dark, dark brown with the tiniest flecks of green in them. He's so close he could kiss me and I want him to. I want him to kiss me more than I've ever wanted anything in my life.

"Evan," I say, and he moves in even closer, then blinks and takes a step back.

"You should probably go." His voice is very quiet.

"What?" I'm still caught in how close he just was, in how badly I wanted him to kiss me—and he wants me to leave?

"Just let yourself out and . . . I don't know. I'll see you around, I guess." He walks off down the hall. After a second I hear a door close.

I should go. He even said I should. I'm scared now, shaking. I definitely should go. What else can I do? I'll leave, I'll drive home, I'll call Dave. Everything will go back to normal then. Everything will be safe.

I walk down the hall.

The minute I do I stop being scared. I know it doesn't make any sense. I should be scared. I've never said anything like the things I've said to Evan tonight. I've never done anything like this. But then I've never wanted to.

Now I do.

He's standing in his room, staring at the wall, and when I walk in he turns around, surprise on his face.

"I thought you were leaving."

"I was going to." I look around his room. It's small and messy. There are clothes on the floor and draped over a chair, stacks of CDs piled against one wall. The closet is open and filled with more CDs and what looks like a couple of keyboards. I dare a quick glance at him and he's watching me, eyes intent on my face.

I look at his desk. It's just a table, one of those small folding ones, and it's piled with books and more CDs and even a few shirts. I walk over and look at the books. At the bottom of one of the piles, turned a little to one side, is a box, faded and a little battered. I reach out and turn it toward me, see the books I was given a long time ago. I see the books I gave him that last awful day, the day I hated what was happening but didn't know what to do. The day I didn't get to say good-bye.

"You kept them," I say, and my voice is shaking. I reach out and trace a finger over the books. My hand is shaking too. I turn around, knowing he's right there, knowing that everything; my heart, my soul, all of me, is in my eyes.

"Lauren," he says, and my name sounds so wonderful, so real, when he says it. I close my eyes, waiting. Hoping. I feel his fingertips touch my face, hear him breathe raggedly, feel his mouth brush against mine.

The moment it does, I know I have never known anything more right.

nineteen

After that everything changed. Evan's mom called when we were twined together, the edge of his desk digging into my hip so hard it left a bruise, but I didn't care, didn't even notice. If she hadn't called I don't know what would have happened. Where things would have gone. I can't really think about it. Or rather I can and I do, but it doesn't even matter. What matters is that when I found the books I'd given him so long ago and turned toward him, I knew what was going to happen. I knew everything was going to change. I knew that and wanted it, wasn't afraid at all.

I watched him talk to his mother, his face flushed, his hair sticking up from my touch, my fingers, and felt this overwhelming wave of happiness rush through me. When he was done telling his mom he was fine, and no, he wasn't out of breath or anything, he was just tired, and yes, he really and truly was okay, and yes, absolutely, he'd call if anything changed, he hung up and we both looked at each other for a moment. Then he grinned, wide and sweet, and just like that I knew he felt the same way too. I knew nothing would be the same.

"She's getting off work in a little while," he said, and I said I should probably go, not sure that I was ready to see Mary again. He walked me to my car and one kiss good-bye turned into many. I couldn't get enough of him, of the sounds he made when I touched him, of the way my skin felt like it was sparking when he touched me. We met up again a day later, snatched an hour in the laundry room of his building when he was washing clothes as punishment for lying about his job and I'd told Dad I'd forgotten something at the grocery store, and by the time I left I felt shaky, drugged from his touch and the feel of his body against mine.

I am used to Dave, to the thrill of wanting to date someone giving way to the reality of it. I wanted Dave to kiss me, but I never felt lost when he did, never feel lost when he does. I sit in my room at night, in front of my computer, messaging with Katie. We talk about clothes and Marcus and homework, and I am looking at my closet and thinking of my mother's things inside it. She was reckless once, more than once, and now I understand why she was. What there is to like about it.

I make plans. I make a cautious plan, a careful one where I will focus on what I have and should be thrilled with, on Dave and how nice he is to me, how lucky I am to be the girl he wants to be with.

I make a reckless plan, a plan where I tell Katie I have practice after school every day for a special concert and so won't need a ride home for a while, a plan where I lie wide-eyed and say, "I know, it's crazy. Honestly, I'm thinking about quitting. But I have to stick it out for at least this term."

Guess which plan I follow through with.

I feel a little nervous when I tell Katie I won't need a ride home from school, but she shrugs and only says something about not getting why I like music so much anyway. Then I feel a little guilty, ask about Harold and Gerald and listen. I don't throw my granola bar wrapper on the floor of her car. I tell myself I am trying to be a good friend.

I know I am not.

When I see Dave I tell him I feel much better and ask lots of questions about John and how he did at his challenge. At lunch I ask about his parents, his training schedule, find out when his first game is. I ask Katie about her nail polish, I ask Marcus about his math class at the community college and pretend I understand something about formulas with letters and numbers in them. I talk and talk, and no one seems to notice anything out of the ordinary. I do, though, and am ashamed of myself.

"So," Dave says, leaning in for a kiss, and I turn so his lips slide across my cheek and not my lips. "Tell me what you did yesterday."

"I—" I say, and I look at him smiling at me. He is so nice, such a great guy. Do I really want to throw what I have with him away because of a few kisses with someone else? Is that the kind of person I am? I have never thought of myself that way. My mother was—is—that way. My father too. But not me. I have seen what reckless does. I am the result of it.

The bell rings, and I don't get a chance to finish my sentence. But I have decided I will change my plan.

I tell Gail this in music, explain what happened with Evan and then say I'm lucky to have Dave. "It would be crazy to throw what we have away, wouldn't it?" I ask as class ends. "I mean, everyone would say that, right?"

She closes her flute case and looks at me. "I don't think I'm the one who needs convincing."

"I don't need convincing. I was just asking if you thought everyone would agree with me about Dave."

"They probably would."

"And you?"

She stands up. "I think what really matters is what you think."

I stare at her, pleading for her to say what I want her to, but she just shrugs. "Fine," I say, and go out into the hallway to meet Katie, holding my hands out for mints.

"You look pissed," she says. "Wintergreen or peppermint?"

"Don't care. Look, about after school today—"

"Yeah?"

"I think I—" We're heading toward the hallway that leads to Axel's class, and as we turn into it I see Evan in front of us. There is a tear in the shoulder of his T-shirt and I can see a hint of skin. I remember how it felt under my fingers. He turns a little, moving to pass someone who is standing in the middle of the hall, and our eyes meet.

"You think what?"

"Nothing," I say. "Just that I have practice, but I already told you that."

"I'm telling you, you should quit," she says. "We'll talk later, okay?"

I nod and walk into Axel's class. To Evan.

In class I pretend I am listening to Axel read from the textbook while sneaking glances at Evan. He doesn't seem to be looking at me, and I feel a horrible wave of panic sweep over me. What if all this, everything I've gotten so worked up over—what if it doesn't mean anything to him?

But there's the way he kisses me. The way he says my name. And the fact that when the bell rings and everyone starts to file out, he does look at me. He looks at me and quietly says, "So I'm going to the library for a while," and I know that he feels everything I do.

I force myself to wait a while before I go to the library. I go to my locker and put all my homework in my bag, even the stuff I know I won't get to, then go to the bathroom and frown over my hair. Then I open my clarinet case and examine all my reeds. Then I frown over my hair some more and finally give up and go to the library.

Evan is waiting outside, leaning against a bulletin board. "Hey."

"I thought—" I gesture at the library door.

"Teacher meeting."

"Oh. So you—"

"Waited. I wasn't sure you'd come. I thought maybe you'd go meet D—"

I don't want him to say it. I don't want to think about anything but the fact that he's here, that I'm here. "There's nowhere else I want to be."

He smiles, and suddenly I can't think about anything but getting him to smile at me like that again.

"So," he says, "while I was waiting, I realized you need to meet my cat."

"What?"

"My cat. You saw her the other night, but, you know, you didn't really get a proper introduction."

"All right," I say, and grin at him. "I'd like to meet your cat."

The cat is waiting for us when we get to Evan's apartment, curled up on the sofa kneading her claws into the fabric.

"Joe," Evan says. "Quit it. We have company."

Joe ignores him.

"Joe? Your cat is named Joe?"

"What? It's a perfectly good name. I'll have you know she loves it."

"Her. You named your cat, your girl cat, Joe?"

He blushes a little. "Hey, I was ten when I got her."

"That's not much of an excuse."

He makes a face at me, and I make one back, and then we are kissing. Joe jumps off the sofa, comes over and glides around our legs. When Evan and I separate, I rest my head on his shoulder, breathing in the scent of his skin.

"So how did you get her?"

"I was riding my bike home from school one afternoon when I heard a noise. It was so quiet, I don't even know how I heard it, but I did. I went to look, and there she was, inside a box just off the side of the road. She was so tiny." He makes a circle in his palm. "I took her home, tried to get her to eat. She was so little she couldn't. When Mom came home I told her I'd found a cat. She practically had a coronary—the apartment we were living in then didn't allow pets—but then she saw Joe." He grins. "She found a vet right away and when we took her in to the vet—he knew what to do, you know? And I thought . . . I wanted to know how to do that. To be like that. So when I go to college—" He breaks off. "That sounded really stupid, right? Because it all sounded pretty stupid to me."

I shake my head. "It sounds great. You're going to be a great vet. I'll have to get a cat just so I can come and see you."

"Yeah?"

"Yeah."

He grins, takes my hand, and walks us both over to the sofa. "So how about you? Big career goals you want to share? It's only fair since I told you mine."

I look at him. He's looking back at me, his eyes dark and intent on my face. Our hands are looped together, resting partially on my folded legs and partially on his. I take a deep breath. And then I tell him the truth.

See, the thing is, I want to be a librarian. Seriously, I do. I don't ever tell anyone that, of course. I say I want to be a fashion designer or doctor or lawyer. It depends on who I'm talking to. Fashion designer is what I told Clara the one time she actually spoke to me, which was at a career day thing right after Dave and I first started dating, and it's what I'll say if any of Dave's friends ever ask me about college (which will never happen). Katie and Dad both think I want to be a lawyer. Dave thinks I want to be a pediatrician.

I told Katie, my father, and Dave what I did because I could tell it was what would make them happy, would fit what they saw when they looked at me. But I tell Evan the truth. I tell him what I really think, really feel. And when I'm done, he smiles at me and says, "I can see that," and then leans closer, gathering my hair in his hands.

"What are you doing?"

He grins more, tucking my hair into a loose bun. "Just seeing what you'll look like as a librarian."

"And?"

"Very hot."

I laugh and press my mouth to his, feel his smile against my own. I hold his hand in mine as we walk to the parking lot later and then drift home, still caught up in my time with him.

This is where I should say I break up with Dave. Or that I stop seeing Evan. But there's nothing to say because I don't do anything. I think about it, tell myself I will figure everything out. That I will do something.

But I don't.

Days bring my usual routine: rides to school with Katie, morning conversations with Dave. Obligatory lunches where freshmen girls watch Dave and me and sigh and Katie stares daggers at Clara if she looks at Marcus. Conversations with Katie about Marcus, about Dave and me, plans for hanging out on the weekend just like always. I listen to myself talk then, and I sound the same. But I don't feel the same.

I feel like I am watching someone else, being someone else, the only real moments in my whole day are the few times my eyes meet Evan's when we pass each other in a hallway, in the conversations Gail and I have where I try to figure out what to do and can never come up with anything.

"Seriously, what do I do?" I ask her for what must be the four hundredth time after jazz band practice one afternoon.

"What do you want to do?"

"I don't know," I say, and that's just it. I don't know. Everything should be easy from this point on. Books and television and movies have told me exactly what to do. I break up with Dave and find happily ever after with Evan.

But it's not that easy. I'm happy with Evan, I am. When I walk into Axel's class and see him, I know what I should do. When I am with him, snatching all the time we can—and it's not enough, it's never enough, every second racing by—I know what I should do. What I want to do. But I can't do it, can't take that step. It's not that easy. Who I am with Evan is—I don't know if it's who I should be. That person, that girl—what will happen to her? I know what will happen to the girl I am with Dave. I know because Dave tells me.

He surprises me one morning, comes by the house as I'm running around frantically, trying to be ready by the time Katie arrives. He rings the doorbell, and I look out the window and see him. I drop the shoes I'm holding and really look at him. His hair is blowing a little in the wind, but it doesn't get messed up, just falls back neatly into place and gleams golden in the sun. He looks like everything I have ever been told to want. He looks up and sees me, waves and smiles. I go downstairs, and he says he has something to show me, makes me close my eyes and walk hand in hand with him down the driveway.

"Okay, open," he says. I open my eyes. He is standing next to a new car. He still shines more than it does.

"It's really nice," I tell him, and look at his hand holding mine as he shows it to me, listen as he outlines plans for our future. Church retreats, trips to the beach with his family in the summer, a walk around a nearby university campus in the fall. Further out, and the car takes us to our last prom, to graduation, to the beach afterward.

"I can even take it with me to college," he says. "I checked and they let freshmen have cars on campus. It'll make it easy for us to come home every weekend."

"Wow," I say faintly.

"It'll be great," he says. "Nothing ever has to change."

I look at him and know he is right. With Dave, everything will unfold just as he's predicted. I may never be popular, may spend the rest of the term, of this year, of high school, being on the fringes, being almost popular but not, but I will be known. I will be his. I will be Dave's Girlfriend. He will treat me with care, with love, and people will see us and think how lucky I am. Who would want to give that up?

I think maybe I would. I think maybe I do.

"Dave—" I say, and the moment I do I know what I want to say next. I want to tell him good-bye. I think I can even say it.

"Wait, wait," he says in a rush. "I know I should have called first, but I really wanted to show you the car and . . ." He looks down at his feet. "Well, I just—this is hard. I came here because I wanted to say that we've been together for a year and a half now and . . . thank you. Thank you for being with me. I'm lucky because you . . . Lauren, you know everything about me. You get me like no one else ever has. You're perfect."

"Me?" I squeak out. "Me?"

"You," he says. "I never told anyone I was seeing that much about me. I never thought anyone would understand how important some stuff is to me. But you, you were so cool with it. The night I told you . . . I wasn't planning on it. But I looked at you, and you were watching me so patiently, like you'd understand anything I said, and I knew. I just knew I could tell you and that you'd get it. With you I think—I think we could have something like my parents do, and that's so amazing to me. I love you."

"Dave," I say again, my voice still squeaky, cracking. He

kisses me before I can say anything else, and as he does I get a look at his eyes. You know what I saw?

He means it. He loves me. He thinks I'm perfect. I am standing in my driveway with no shoes on, and I'm not perfect, am so far from perfect. But he thinks I am. He is happy with me.

I couldn't make my mother happy. My father—he tries, but I am a reminder of his failures, a living monument to someone he had and could never really hold. Dave is the first person who ever looked at me like I could bring joy.

And so nothing changes. It makes me a terrible person. I know that. But what is in my heart for Evan is wild, unknown, and what I have with Dave is easy. Safe. And I can't choose between them. I am too unsure. Too scared of what will happen to me if I do. I am not strong or brave or anything like I should be. I am just me.

twenty

On Saturday morning Evan and I go grocery shop-ping. I spent last night at a party, stood watching people walk by and talk to Dave and nod at me as long as Dave's arm rested lightly around my shoulders. I drank beer and watched people hook up. I listened to Marcus talk about some summer thing he and Dave wanted to do, smiled brightly at Katie whenever she asked if I was okay. I thought the night would never end, stood there bored and thinking about Evan.

"Are you sure there's nothing you want to tell me?" Katie asked at one point, when the two of us had gone to use the bathroom. We'd actually gone outside. She asked me as she was checking on Harold and Gerald, one hand over her cell phone, her eyes intent on my face, like she knew exactly what—who—I'd been thinking about all evening.

"What do you mean?"

"You just—hold on. Harold," she said into the phone, "that's so great! No, don't go ask Mom. Just put it up on the fridge. The tape is on the counter where I keep the bills. Yep, in the basket. Put Gerald on, please." She put one hand over the phone again. "You just seem—Hi, Gerald. No, I'm not mad. I know you worked really hard on it. Of course you're still going to karate tomorrow. Yes, I promise. Tell Harold I want to talk to him again." She sighed, rubbed one hand across her forehead.

"You all right?" I asked, and she nodded at me.

"Harold, what did I tell you about teasing Gerald about karate? No, I don't think that's what I said. Do you want to stay home tomorrow? Good. Now apologize. Yes, I'm waiting." She rubbed her head again. "Okay, thank you. Please don't stay up too late and don't—that's right. Mom likes the television quiet. Okay. Bye."

"God," she said when she'd hung up and rubbed her hand across her forehead again. I realized her fingers were shaking.

"Hey," I said, and looped one arm through hers. "What's going on?"

"Nothing really. Mom's just . . . feeling worse than usual, that's all."

"I'm sorry."

She sighed. "Me too. What was I just saying before—?" She pointed at her phone.

"Don't remember," I lied. "Is there anything I can do?"

She shook her head and then rested it against my shoulder. "Let's just go back inside." So we did, and I felt like shit for being relieved that all the crap Katie was dealing with made her forget about the question she'd asked me.

But I did feel relieved, and when I wake up all I can think about is how I'm going to see Evan soon, how we're going to spend the whole day together. He looks mostly asleep when I pick him up, is standing outside his apartment complex waiting for me, leaning against a stop sign with his eyes more than half closed.

"Hey," I say, and he opens them slowly, blinks at me, and then smiles.

"Hey."

"You look kind of tired."

"That's because it's barely morning."

"Are you sure you want to come?"

"It's you," he says softly. "Of course I want to come."

I lean over and kiss him when he gets in the car. He looks rumpled and wonderful. I pass him the coffee I made him.

"Do I get to keep the mug?"

I laugh, and we drive to the grocery store. I haven't been in a grocery store with anyone in a long time, and shopping with him is fun. I learn he likes apples but not oranges, that he can make an omelet, and that he doesn't quite get the importance of stocking up on super fancy ice cream when it's on sale.

"It'll take you a month to eat all this," he says as I put another pint of chocolate chocolate chip in the cart. "And that's if all you eat is ice cream three times a day, every day. You do know they aren't going to run out, right?"

"Ha ha. It's on sale. It's a bargain."

"Four dollars a pint is on sale? Wait, did I just say that? Shit. I sounded like my mom." He starts tossing more ice cream in the cart. "Quick, buy more! Buy lots! It's a bargain!"

I laugh and shut the freezer door. He stands behind me and places his hands over mine on the cart, twining our fingers together. "So now what?"

"Now we're done. And if you're really nice, I'll let you come home with me and help put everything away."

"Man, you do know how to show a guy a good time."

"I try."

He laughs, kisses my neck, and then yawns. "I didn't know grocery stores were open this early."

"It's not that early. Besides, the best time to go is in the morning, before it gets busy and stuff." Before anyone we go to school with could possibly see us.

He moves away from me a bit, his fingers starting to slide away from mine, and I look back at him. He's not smiling, and I know he realizes what I'm doing. I look away, stare at the magazines and pretend their covers fascinate me. One of them has a headline in huge letters, "Boyfriend Alert: Is He Cheating on You?"

No, but I'm cheating on him. I'm cheating on my boyfriend. I'm not perfect, but I never thought I'd do something like this. Is this who I want to be?

I don't know.

I don't know, but I don't let go of Evan's hands. Instead I

look down at them and stroke my fingers over his knuckles, watch as his fingers stiffen, then relax and twine around mine again. After I pay for the groceries we drive back to my house and put them away. We eat ice cream and talk about everything—school, movies, music, books. I can talk to Evan about anything. Anything except one thing. We don't talk about Dave and me. I can tell he wants to and I know we should but I just—I don't know what to do. I should, I know, but I don't. I don't even want to think about it. I push everything away, focus only on Evan and how happy he makes me, but that night, when Evan goes to the hospital to help with a blood drive his mother is coordinating, it's all I can think about.

It's all I can think about because I'm sitting in Dave's house, eating dinner with his parents and John.

"You want some more carrots?" Dave asks. I shake my head. He smiles at me. He's smiling at me and I'm cheating on him. I think of all the fights I've seen about it at school, at parties. I think about how everyone dissects everything afterward. I think about things I've heard people say. I think about things I've said. If Dave were doing this to me . . .

Dave would never do this to me.

I excuse myself and go to the bathroom. I don't look in the mirror, just put my hands on the counter and stare down at them. I can hear Dave and his family talking.

"I was just telling everyone I volunteer with about you two," his mother says. "I promised to bring in pictures next time."

"Mom," Dave says, but his voice is light, teasing. "Next

thing I know you'll be asking me to stop by and bring Lauren with me so you can show us both off."

"Well, I'm proud of you, and I think you've got a wonderful girlfriend. What's wrong with that?" Her voice is teasing too, full of love for him.

"She is pretty wonderful," Dave says, and I hear his mother murmur her agreement, his father do the same. John asks for the potatoes, and I flush the toilet and wash my hands, noise to make it seem like I haven't been standing in here unable to look at myself in the mirror. I catch a glimpse of myself as I'm drying my hands. I don't think I look wonderful at all.

But I'll try, I tell myself after Dave has dropped me off. I keep thinking of that magazine headline, of Evan looking at me and knowing why we were out so early, of how he didn't ask what I was doing tonight when he left. I think about Dave smiling at me. I think about him telling his family how wonderful I am. I brush my teeth, look in the mirror at my mother's eyes, and think about what she did to my father. I think about what she did to me. She knew how to hurt people. She was good at it. I don't have to be like that.

So I try. On Sunday I go to church with Dad in the morning, and then spend the whole day with Katie, invite her over and turn my cell off, tell her I'm just letting the answering machine pick up when the phone rings. I don't trust myself to talk to Evan. Not yet. Tomorrow I will talk to him. Tomorrow I will tell him—I don't know.

"What don't you know?" I look up and Katie is watching me, a puzzled look on her face.

"What?"

"You said you don't know. So what don't you know?"

"Oh, just—" I point at my homework. "It doesn't make any sense."

She nods, goes back to her own books. I stare down at my notebook, at my pen doodling circles across it. I could tell her I don't feel well and call Evan when she leaves. I could go downstairs and talk to Dad, have him grunt at me when I ask him how he is, and then come back up and tell her something's come up and that I'll call her in a few hours. Then I can call and tell her things are weird, that I'll just see her tomorrow. She'd understand. I could even—I could just say I was going to go grab something, McDonald's or whatever, and not come back for a while, say there was a long line or that I forgot money and had to go to an ATM. I wish I could just leave and not worry about it. I wish I could go and not come back. I wish—

Now I know how my mother felt, what she must have thought before she left. *I wish I could just leave.* Oh God. I won't do that. I won't be that.

"So what's going on with you and Marcus?" I ask, and listen when Katie talks. I listen and I don't leave. I won't.

In school on Monday I throw myself into what I have. I am smiling and cheerful when I see Dave, spend lunch talking to him and Katie and Marcus. This is good, I tell myself. This is who I'm supposed to be. I pull my chair closer to Dave's, think about him saying how wonderful I am. I look out the window as we're leaving, heading back to our classes, and see Gail outside, walking in from the parking lot. She is smiling, and I can tell, just from her smile, that she skipped out on lunch to see Jennie.

I squeeze Dave's hand, lean in and kiss him, tell him I'll see him later. I look back over at Gail. She looks so happy. I duck into the bathroom, Katie right behind me talking away. I stand in front of a sink, look into the mirror and pretend to fix my hair. I am smiling, but the smile on my face looks nothing like the one on Gail's.

"I haven't seen you so happy in ages," Katie says, and I watch my smiling mouth turn up wider. I feel completely empty inside.

But I'm doing the right thing, I fake cramps to get out of music and world history, hide out in the nurse's office till school is over. When the final bell rings, I head off to find Katie and get a ride home. Maybe I'll even tell her I'll go with her to pick up her brothers, keep myself busy until—until later.

But when I find Katie at her locker, what I say is, "Hey, I forgot I've got a stupid dentist appointment today. I gotta go meet Dad out front. You know how he is about having to take time off work."

She gives me a sympathetic smile and says, "Okay, call me later." I say I will and walk away.

Then I go to the library.

Evan is there. I see him when I walk in, sitting at a table in the back, and the moment I do I feel such a sense of relief, of happiness, that I realize everything I've told myself I want and that I'll do isn't what I want at all.

I walk over to him, smile when he looks up and sees me.

"Hey," he says. His voice is quiet, cautious. He isn't smiling.

"Hey," I say. "Can I sit down?"

"You sure you want to?"

"I'm sure."

He nods. He still isn't smiling. "Really? Because I didn't talk to you yesterday, haven't seen you today. I thought maybe you might be avoiding me, that maybe you and Da—"

"No," I say, starting to lie, and then stop. "I mean, I was avoiding you. But not because of . . ."

"I know his name."

"I know that," I say, biting my lip. "But it's not because of him. It's me. I was just—I was trying to figure stuff out."

"Did you?"

"I think so," I say, and dare to sit down, to slide my hand across the table toward his. Please, I think, *please*, and am dizzy with relief, with joy, when our fingers touch, when he moves his hand across mine, a caress.

"I missed you," I tell him. He smiles then, really smiles.

"I missed you too," he says, and I may be a horrible person. But I am happy.

We stay in the library for a while, pretending to do homework but mostly making out in the reference section. As we're leaving, walking across the parking lot together, I hear someone call Evan's name. We both turn, and Marcus is a few rows away, standing by his car.

"Hey, man," he says to Evan. "I thought I saw you." He gives me an unreadable glance. "Hey, Lauren."

"Hey," Evan and I both say, and then Marcus says something to Evan, and Evan says something back, but I don't hear it because I'm not listening. I'm too busy thinking about what would have happened if Katie had been with him. Evan and I aren't holding hands or anything, but Katie—Katie would have guessed what's going on, I'm sure.

"So I guess I'll see you around," Evan says, his shoulder brushing against mine and snapping me out of my thoughts.

Marcus nods. "Yeah, see you." He shoots me another look and then gets in his car. I wonder if he'll tell Katie.

I don't know if I hope he will or not. Sometimes being me is very confusing.

"Hey there," Evan says, waving a hand in front of my face. "You okay?"

"Yeah." I nod. "I just didn't know you and Marcus are, you know, friends."

Evan shrugs. "I worked with his dad at Anderson, and Marcus came in and worked a shift a couple of times."

"Marcus? But I thought his family was . . . I didn't know his dad worked—"

"Not everyone's father designs bazillion-dollar houses for a living."

"That's not—I just. I didn't know," I say. "Katie's never said anything."

"Maybe she doesn't know."

"Maybe," I say, but then I remember her telling me that Marcus needs a scholarship to go to college. I remember the day after Evan and I first kissed, she told me Marcus had to go home because his dad got hurt. . . . "The night you hurt your hand, did anyone else get hurt?"

"Yeah. The same pallet that hit"—he holds out his hand—"caught Marcus's dad on the arm. Tore a big gash. It was really nasty looking. They actually wanted him to go to the hospital but . . ." He shrugs.

"But what?"

"He couldn't. He doesn't have insurance."

"But if he works there full time he would . . ." I trail off, thinking of Evan's job with Anderson. "He works there like—like you did."

Evan nods. "He used to work at some plant, but he said it closed a few years ago and after that working at Anderson was the only job he could find."

"Wow." I always thought that Marcus's life was just like Dave's, that he never had anything to really worry about. I mean, he has a car, he plays football, he's popular. "Did . . . did they fire him too?"

"Yeah," Evan says. "They did. Marcus says he's looking for work but there aren't a lot of options around here."

"But he's okay, right? I mean, his arm, it's better?"

Evan nods. "If that pallet had been a couple of inches farther along, though . . ." He shakes his head. "It could have been a lot worse."

It could have been Evan. He could have been standing where Marcus's dad was. He could have hurt more than his hand. If things had been just a little different—

"It could have been you," I say, and my voice is shaking. I reach out, take his hand. I don't care that we're in the parking lot. I look down at his fingers, at his bitten nails, the almost faded bruises. "You could have been . . . you could have been really hurt. You could have been—"

"Hey," he says gently. "I'm okay. And I promise that if I ever find another job I'll be extra careful."

"Another job?" My voice is still shaking.

"Yeah, once Mom gets through making me volunteer at the hospital to make up for lying to her—I've only got two weeks left after today—I've got to get one. I mean, I've got college coming up and I doubt I'm going to be winning any scholarships so—"

"But can't your mom help?"

"Yeah, but she has her own college loans to pay off. She says it doesn't matter, but I don't want her to owe more on account of me."

"You . . . you won't try to work somewhere like Anderson again, right?"

"Three guesses as to who you sound like. I'll give you a hint. Three letters, O in the middle."

"Very funny. I'm serious."

"I'm being serious too. You totally sound like my mom."

"Evan! I just—I don't want you to get hurt."

"You shouldn't worry about me."

"I can't help it. I like you, you . . . jackass."

"Really?" he says, grinning, and leans in.

"Yes, really," I tell him, and then he kisses me, right there in the parking lot. And I kiss him back.

twenty-one

The next afternoon Evan scribbles something in his notebook as Axel is talking about the papal states. I am trying to listen but am mostly thinking about pizza and how the school cafeteria always ruins it. It should be impossible to mess up bread, tomato sauce, and cheese, but yet they always do. Axel scrapes chalk across the blackboard, grinding out someone's name and, I swear, smiling as we all wince. Evan turns his notebook toward me.

"Don't have to go to the hospital today," it says. "Want to go somewhere?"

I nod, and he shoves his hair back from his forehead with one hand and grins at me. I grin back and start waiting for class to end.

It takes forever, of course, and when it finally does, both Katie and Marcus are waiting by my locker.

"Hey," I say, surprised. "What's going on?"

"Marcus actually has a free afternoon," Katie tells me, grinning. "So I was thinking that maybe . . ."

I grin back at her, elated. For once I don't have to think of a lie or anything. "Sure," I say, "I can get someone to give me a ride home."

"Dave could probably take you," Marcus says. He looks down toward Dave's locker, starts to call his name.

"It's okay," I say hastily. "I've got some stuff to do so I'll probably be a while. And"—I look down at Dave, who waves at me with a strange, distracted look on his face—"I'm sure he wants to go straight home. John has a big skills challenge coming up."

"I thought he already had that," Marcus says. When I glance over at him, wondering if I've heard something in his voice, he's looking at Katie, smiling at her like she's the whole world. Before I always found how they were around each other slightly (fine, more than slightly) annoying. But now I get it.

"Oh, you know how it is," I say as lightly as I can, and then shut my locker. "They're both always doing something. I'll see you later."

Katie says good-bye. Marcus doesn't say anything. I turn back to look at them at the end of the hallway. Katie is rummaging through her bag and doesn't see me, but Marcus does. I give him a quick hey-everything-is-fine smile. He smiles back, but the smile doesn't quite reach his eyes.

I don't really have time to think about it though, and honestly, I wouldn't even if I did because Evan is waiting for me in the library. After half an hour of him doing homework and me asking him where we're going and not getting an answer, we finally head to his car.

"I can't believe you won't tell me where we're going," I say as we pull out of the school parking lot.

"I can't believe you just spent half an hour asking me the same question over and over again."

"Hey!" I say, and stick my tongue out at him. "So how come you didn't bring any books with you? I mean, not that I didn't enjoy the tour of your locker, but there's no way you could have gotten all your homework done."

"I never do homework at home," he says. "Well, okay. On the weekend sometimes. But when I was working at Anderson, the last thing I wanted to do when I was actually at home was homework, and I just got into the habit of not doing it there."

"So when do you do it?"

"What, you don't think I can get it all done in half an hour?" I roll my eyes at him and he laughs. "I do it at lunch and after school."

"Oh." Now I guess I know why I've never seen him leaving any of the lunch periods in spite of my occasional—well, perhaps slightly more than that—checking. "So you don't eat lunch with anyone? At all?"

"Hey, I've smelled that crap they call pizza, and I'm pretty sure I'm not missing out on anything."

I laugh and tell him I was thinking about that earlier. But

I feel kind of sorry for him too, wonder why he doesn't eat with anyone. I don't know how to ask about it though.

"What?" he says.

I shake my head at him.

"You're thinking something, I can tell."

"It's nothing, really. Just—" Forget it, I don't know how to ask. It must be hard, to be at a new school. Before Dave and Marcus, Katie and I ate lunch by ourselves. It was just easier than running the gauntlet of tables and trying to find somewhere to sit. "Where are we going?"

"You'll see."

"I hope you know I'm going to keep asking till you tell me."

"Fine with me. I like the sound of your voice."

I try not to act like I've melted into a little pile of goo, but really. He just does things to me.

We end up driving all the way out to Suffolk, which is the home of Suffolk University. Katie and I come out here sometimes, to go shopping and look at all the cute college guys. Suffolk is really cool, this small town that's full of neat little restaurants and bookstores that smell like books and not like carpet cleaner and coffee. Evan and I go to a couple of the bookstores, walk hand in hand through the aisles. I notice, when we're in the second one, that people seem to know who he is. A lot of people. People-in-college kind of people. I know he used to live here, but this is beyond that. I don't ask about it until he takes me inside a music shop where everyone, from the clerks to every single person thumbing through the display bins, says hello to him and asks what he's been up to.

"So I guess you must come here a lot," I say.

He looks over at me as he thumbs through a pile of CDs, grinning as he finds one and pulls it out. "Sort of."

"Hey, Evan," someone says, and I look up to see an absolutely gorgeous (and college-aged) girl grinning at him.

"Hey," he says, smiling back at her, and I'm jealous. I've never been jealous before, ever, but right now I totally get why Katie hates Clara so much. Totally.

"This is Lauren," he says to the girl, and then wraps an arm around my waist, pulling me close.

"Oh," the girl says, sounding disappointed. She smiles at me—in a teeth-baring grimace kind of way—and then wanders off. I pluck the CD that Evan is holding out of his hands and then kiss him.

"What was that for?" he says. "Whatever it was, please tell me so I can do it again."

"Shut up," I mutter, but I don't mean it and he knows it because he is smiling at me.

We stop and grab something to eat after he buys his CD, sandwiches in a little deli right by the campus where, once again, everyone seems to know who he is.

"Okay," I say when we are back in the car, heading home. "I know you used to live there and everything, but how did all those college students know you?"

"Well, see, I'm really a college student posing as a high school student—"

I swat him on the arm. "Seriously."

"I wasn't really into the whole high school thing but the band I was in, we used to play on campus a lot so—"

"So that's how come gorgeous women come up to you and say hello like they want you to come back to their place with them?"

He laughs, looks over at me. "That's what all that was about? Man, if only I'd known. We're going back every chance we get from now on."

I raise my eyebrows at him, and he laughs again. "You're cute when you're jealous."

"You're supposed to say I'm cute all the time."

"Okay. You're cute all the time."

"It doesn't count if you say it after I tell you to."

He grins at me. "How about if I say it now?"

"Maybe," I tell him, smiling back. "So if you were Mr. Popular in Suffolk, then how come I never see you talking to anyone at school?"

"I talk to people," he says, and then laughs at the look I give him.

"I do," he says. "Just—I don't know. This is my third high school in three years, and it's been the same bullshit in each one. You'd think something would be different but nothing ever is. Everyone has their little groups, and everything is all about who's doing what and who they're doing it with, and between work and everything else it just . . . it all seems so pointless." He shrugs, then looks over at me. "Does that make sense?"

I think about the night Dave and I met everyone for pizza and I stood in the bathroom watching all the girls talk, part of a group but not part of it at all. I think about how bored I was and how good leaving felt. I think about how I've felt at parties lately, as if they're a chore I have to get through. I think about how lunch has seemed to become longer and more annoying every day.

"Yeah," I tell him. "It does."

We stop for gas right before we reach our exit. While he's fiddling with the pump I go inside and buy a slushee for myself and a jumbo soda for him. He smiles as I hand him the enormous cup and when he kisses me, he tastes so sweet. The thing about Evan's kisses is that every single one makes the whole world seem to tilt a little. Makes me feel so alive. It's the most amazing feeling.

twenty-two

When I get home Dad is there. He is there because he is packing. He tells me he's going out of town tonight. "Emergency meeting in the morning," he says. "There's some developers pitching an idea for a community, and they heard about the work I did on the Seabrook Farms development last year—you remember that?—and so I'm going in to consult with them. It's a big opportunity."

I nod. "How long will you be gone?"

"Two days. Three at the most."

"Do you need me to pick you up at the airport? Or take you there?"

He shakes his head.

"Okay," I say, and then we both stand there, silent.

"So I should—" I say at the same time he says, "I keep thinking we should talk."

"About what?" I say, and as he shifts his weight from one foot to another I know he isn't going to say anything else.

"I'm fine, Dad," I tell him. I try to make my voice sound bright, but I think it mostly just comes out as tired. "I'm totally fine."

"I want more for you than that. I want you to be happy."

"I'll work on it," I tell him, and force a smile to my face. "Did you leave a number?"

He nods. "And if you need anything—"

"I know, I'll call. You want me to make you a sandwich or something? You could eat it on your way to the airport."

He says that would be nice, so I make him a sandwich. He forgets to take it with him.

I turn off my cell after he leaves, ignore the phone when it rings. I don't want to talk to anyone right now, not even Evan. Thinking about Dad and how he said he wanted to talk when he knew he was leaving, when he knew he had no time for me, has left me feeling sad and angry and I just want to be alone.

The thing is, when I try to go to sleep it's so quiet, too quiet, and every breath I take sounds like a scream. I get out of bed and sit on the floor, looking through my box of Mom's things.

"I don't miss you at all," I tell her high school picture. She stares out at me radiant, smiling. She doesn't call me a liar. She doesn't answer.

* * *

I'm exhausted the next morning, all my classes a blur. I avoid everyone and even skip lunch, hide out in the guidance office pretending to look at college brochures. Gail and I talk a little during music, although Mr. Herrity glares at us and so the conversation never gets much farther than me asking about her dress for the dance and her telling me I look tired. I avoid Katie afterward by ducking outside and walking around to the wing of the school where Axel's class is, bumping into someone as I head inside.

"Sorry," I mumble, and look up to see Evan in front of me, concern on his face, in his eyes.

"You look like you need to get out of here," he says.

So we do. We get in his car and leave. We go to the movies, eat popcorn, and watch a skinny beautiful blonde girl play an ugly duckling high school student who's transformed by love. I laugh at the total unbelievability of a girl like that being an ugly duckling, ask Evan if he thinks people who make movies ever actually went to high school, and then fall asleep, only waking up when the lights come back on at the end.

"I fell asleep," I say.

"Yep."

"Was the rest of the movie as bad as the first ten minutes?"

"Worse," Evan says with a smile. "She made a speech at the end about following your heart and then got crowned prom queen."

"I'm sorry."

"Don't be," he says, and smoothes my hair back from my face with one hand. I smile when strands of it catch on his fingers.

"I don't have prom queen hair."

"Sure you do. And you drool when you sleep too."

"I do not!"

"You do. It's cute."

I make a face at him, and he leans over and kisses me. "You feel better?

"Yeah."

"Good," he says, and stands up, reaches out for my hand. "Come on."

We head out to his car. There are only a few cars in the parking lot, most of them way down at the far end, and as I look out the windshield it's easy to pretend we're the only people in the world, just us floating in a strange concrete sea.

"So, thanks for the movie," I tell him, glad we've agreed we don't have to leave just yet. "And the popcorn. Next time I buy though, okay?"

"Only if you promise to fall asleep and drool on me again."

"I didn't drool on you!"

He points at his shoulder. "Right here. Check it out."

"I don't see anything."

He grins at me. "Look closer."

"And then what? I'm all close to you and what, become overwhelmed and start making out with you?"

"Hey, it worked in the movie."

"Yeah?" I say, and move a little closer.

"Yeah," he says, and I smile as his mouth meets mine.

We make out in the car for a long time, so long that all the windows fog up. I trace my name across one of them when we've separated for a moment, leaning back and watching my finger glide across the cool glass.

"I hope you know that didn't happen in the movie," he says, kissing my ear.

"Really?" I shiver a little, my hand falling away from the window and sliding across his shoulder. "So what did happen?"

"Duh." He grins at me. "She and the big football star made out and then talked about their feelings."

I laugh. "That sounds about right. Actually, the sad thing is that with Dave that totally would be what would . . ." I trail off, aware that Evan has moved away from me.

"Sorry," I say, and reach for him.

"It's okay," he says, but he sure doesn't sound like he means it and moves even farther away. "It's just . . . Well, talk about the boyfriend is, you know, great for the old ego. Especially during—" He gestures at the still slightly foggy windows.

"Dave's not—" I break off before I can finish, before I say "my boyfriend" and lie. Because as much as I don't want him to be right now, he still is.

"He's not?" Evan has moved closer now, is smiling at me. "When did you break up with him?"

"I—"

"You haven't," he says, his smile fading. "Of course you haven't. Why would you want to give up Mr. Wonderful?"

"Evan—"

"Let me ask you something. What am I? Something to do when he's busy?"

"No! I don't even want to be with him. I want to be with you. I just . . . it's complicated."

"Complicated. Like, you making sure he doesn't find out about me complicated, right?"

"It's not like that! I didn't plan this and I'm just . . . you make me happy. So happy I'm—" I take a deep breath and stare down at my feet. "I'm scared. The way I feel around you . . . I've never felt like it before."

Evan is silent. After a moment I glance over at him. He's looking at me. I want to reach out and touch him, but I'm afraid he'll push me away. I don't want that—I'm terrified of it—but I can't help myself when it comes to him, and so even though my hand is shaking, I reach out, trace my fingers across his jaw. I say his name, watch his eyes flutter closed.

"I get it," he says quietly, and then opens his eyes. "The first couple of times I gave you a ride home, the first couple of times we talked, I—it was like I couldn't let myself think about it, you know? And then after the night I hurt my hand I just . . . I knew you were with Dave and I hated it, but it made me feel better too. It meant I didn't have to worry about liking you too much, that whatever was going on was because you were bored or Dave was busy or whatever."

"Evan . . ." I say, stung.

"That's what I told myself, anyway," he continues. "But it wasn't like that. It never was. I know that. When I'm with you it's—"

"Special," I say, and he nods, leans forward so our foreheads are resting together.

"It's amazing," he whispers, and I close my eyes and kiss him.

After the windows fog up again and the sun starts to set, we get something to eat and then drive back to school. I look at Dad's car, sitting lonely in the parking lot, and think about what's waiting for me at home. Nothing. Absolutely nothing except maybe messages from Katie and Dave that I won't want to return. I wish this afternoon could have lasted forever. I wish—I sigh, start to pull on my jacket and open the car door.

"Hey," Evan says, and when I look over at him he's biting his lip, looking nervous. "Mom's going to be working really late tonight. Do you—do you want to go back to my place for a while?"

"Yes," I say without hesitation. We could go to my house but I don't want to. I want to get away from it, from its emptiness, from who I am there. I want to go to Evan's. I feel alive there, with him. I feel real.

He looks at me, his eyes intent, dark and beautiful, and I know what I've said means, I do. But I'm okay with it. I want to be with him more than I've ever wanted anything before.

Joe is waiting for us when we get to the apartment, winding around our ankles and purring hello before heading into the kitchen. Evan feeds her and then comes back, smiling when he sees I'm still standing in the middle of the living room.

"You can sit down, you know."

"I know." You'd think with all the stuff I've heard from Katie—and hell, seen at parties—I wouldn't be so nervous. But I am. I want to be with Evan, I do. Maybe I should be worried about ending up like my mom, but I'm not. I take birth control pills, I have condoms, I'm prepared. What's getting to me is that now that we're here it—*it*—is all I can think about. What will it be like to be that close with someone? It's kind of completely overwhelming.

"I promise it's totally safe. I mean, I have lost a couple of pairs of socks in there and there was that bag of corn chips that disappeared. . . ."

I look over at him, and he's grinning at me. I make a face at him and flop onto the sofa, then throw a decorative pillow that has been mauled by Joe's claws at his head. "You know, laughing at me isn't really—"

"What?"

"You know." I glance over at the hallway, back toward his room, and feel my face heat.

He sits down next to me, clears his throat. "Look, I'm—" He breaks off.

"What?"

"I don't know." He laughs, his face a little flushed. "Usually I can think of something to say, but now—" He makes a 'nothing' gesture with one hand.

"You're blushing," I say, and start to giggle.

"Nice," he says, and now his face is bright red. "Exactly how I pictured this going."

"You pictured this?"

He looks over at me, eyebrows raised. I look back at him, and he turns even brighter red.

"What? I'm a guy. It's what we do. I mean, not that I'm some sort of—oh, hell."

"Sweet talker." I lean in toward him, hear his breath catch. It makes mine catch too.

"Lauren," he says, barely a whisper, and I could listen to him say my name forever. Then he touches me, and I want that to last forever too.

Not that everything is perfect. The sofa is kind of narrow and either my legs or Evan's keep sliding off it. I can't seem to unbutton his shirt either—never mind that I've been perfectly able to work buttons every other moment of my life—and I find myself wishing I'd worn any other bra besides my plain boring white one. But in spite of all of this, or maybe because of it, it all feels that much more real. I'm conscious of everything, of Evan's hands on my skin, of his mouth, of the way he is looking at me and how it makes me feel and now—

Now I hear something. Evan and I look at each other, and there is very definitely the sound of someone outside, of a key turning. The two of us spring apart, and I push myself up, start to fix my bra, and then settle for pulling my shirt closed. I fold my arms across my chest in what I hope is an I-swear-I-haven't-been-rolling-around-on-the-sofa kind of way.

The door opens and Mary walks in, dropping a bag on the floor and heading directly for the kitchen. She looks exactly like I remembered and yet nothing like it at the same time. Her face is the same, but there are wrinkles around her eyes and mouth. She must have been so young when she was with Dad. I never realized that. Her hair is different too, longer and streaked a dark red, but her smile is still the same, and I realize with a shock that it is like Evan's, that they share the same wide radiant grin.

"God, what a madhouse," she calls out, still smiling and heading toward the kitchen. "I know you're holed up in your room pretending to do homework, but you have to hear this. Four nurses already called in sick for tomorrow, so guess who has to stay at work and fill in? I'm just here to grab a change of clothes and then . . ." She trails off, looks over at the sofa. At Evan and me sitting on the sofa.

"Lauren?" she says, her voice stunned.

"Hi, Mar—Mrs.—hi," I say.

"Well, I didn't expect—Look at you," she says. Her smile is back but not quite as wide, not quite as real. "How are you?"

"I'm good. How—how are you?"

"All right," she says with a little almost-laugh. "Busy. Wow, it's such a surprise to see you. It's been a really long time, hasn't it?" She's definitely not smiling now, and I know who she is thinking about.

"It has," I say tentatively. She shakes her head, and the not quite real smile from before is back on her face.

"I wish I could stay and catch up, but I've got to get back to work. However, if you find out who Evan's seeing, you'll have to let me know, okay? He won't tell me anything about her."

Evan tenses, and I see Mary take in his rumpled shirt. My rumpled shirt.

"Oh," she says flatly. "I see. But . . . Mrs. Hall, one of our volunteers, she's always talking about you, her son Dave's great girlfriend. She even mentioned you when I ran into her yesterday. I guess she doesn't know you two broke up yet?"

I look down at the floor.

There's silence for a moment, and then Mary sighs. "Just like your father," she says softly, and the way she says it, without any surprise at all, destroys me.

"Mom," Evan says, but I'm already pushing off the sofa and heading for the door, my face burning, her words ringing in my ears.

Outside I fumble with my shirt, buttoning it as I race down the stairs. *Just like your father*. She's right. God, she's so right. I never—I was so worried about being like Mom that I never realized I'm just like Dad too. He always had another girlfriend lined up, always moved on to someone new before the person he supposedly loved knew he didn't love her anymore. Everything that's horrible in my parents—I got all of it. Every last rotten bit.

I bite my lip hard, willing my eyes to stop stinging, and head quickly across the parking lot, cross onto the road. The school is a long way away, but I can walk there. I have to. I can't go back to the apartment, not now, not ever again. A car honks as it whizzes by me and I move farther over to the side of the road, the ground a blur in front of me. I never cry, ever, but my eyes are watering and these weird noises are ripping up my throat and rolling out of me, and I can't stop it. I stand there, my whole body shaking, and cry for the first time in years.

"Lauren!"

Oh God, it's Evan. I look over my shoulder and see him walking toward me. I look back at the ground and squeeze my eyes shut, trying to stop the tears. It doesn't work.

I hear him stop a few feet away from me, and when he

speaks his voice is faint over the sounds of passing cars. "I'm sorry."

My eyes fly open, and I turn around, staring at him. "What?"

"I'm sorry," he says again, and moves closer, reaching out like he's going to touch me.

"No," I say, and take a step back. "You—you shouldn't say that. You don't need to. I do. I'm sorry. I'm—I've been so afraid that I'm like my mom, that I'm going to do the same things she did, that I didn't realize I'm just like my dad. I'm just like both of them and I'm—" I'm crying even harder now, stand there feeling raw and broken and unable to stop myself from saying what I fear is true. "I'm awful."

"You aren't awful."

"I am." I am crying so hard now I can hardly breathe.

"You aren't."

I shake my head and turn away, not wanting him to look at me. I'm not worth looking at.

"Hey," he says, and reaches out, turns me around to face him. "Look at me. We aren't them, Lauren. You're not your mother or father any more than I'm my mother. You're you and I'm me and I love you."

I stop crying. Did he just— "What did you say?"

"I love you."

"Evan," I say, "Evan," and then he is kissing me and I am kissing him, and we are heading back to the apartment, to where it will be just the two of us, and if it's reckless or wrong or both I don't care. I'm with him and it's exactly where I want to be.

twenty-three

Evan drives me to school early the next morning. It takes me quite a while to get out of his car, and when I finally get into mine, I realize how late it is. I drive home and take the world's fastest shower, then call Katie and tell her not to worry, that she doesn't have to pick me up. When she starts asking questions I say, "I've got to go," and hang up. Everything with Evan is wonderful. But everything else—I don't know. I just don't know. I look in the mirror and sigh. My hair is never going to be anything but straight and boring, is it?

But Evan likes it. I smile at that, my mind drifting away. When I finally notice what time it is, I'm running very late. As in school-will-be-starting-in-just-a-few-minutes late. I curse and finish getting ready as fast as I can, then race out to the car.

I get to school just before the first period bell is about to ring. No sign of Dave, which is good. But no sign of Evan either. Damn. I head toward my locker and stop because Katie is there, leaning against the one next to mine.

"Hey," she says.

"Hey. If you're looking for Marcus, I haven't seen him, but you can probably find him before the bell . . ." I trail off. Katie is looking at me, and it isn't a particularly nice look.

"What?" I say, and open my locker, stare inside so I don't have to see her.

"So I was talking to Marcus last night," she says. "And he told me the funniest thing. Remember the afternoon you said you had to go to the dentist? Marcus told me he saw you and Evan in the parking lot. He said he talked to you two for a minute and then left, only he had to come right back because he forgot something. You two were still there."

I close my locker and look at her. I think she knows what's going on.

"We need to talk," she tells me.

She definitely knows.

I don't go to first period. Katie and I go the bathroom instead, the one where the pot smokers hang out. This early in the morning only two of them are there, and they're both asleep. One of them has a half-empty bag of cheese puffs resting next to her. My stomach rumbles.

"Didn't get a chance to eat breakfast," I tell Katie, trying a shaky smile. "And hey, I'm sorry I called so late this morning. I just—I got distracted."

"I bet," she says, and her voice is colder than I've ever heard it.

"You know about Evan and me," I say cautiously, and she nods. "Are you mad?"

"Am I mad? Am I MAD? I find out from Marcus—Marcus!—that my best friend is kissing a guy who isn't her boyfriend in the parking lot, and then spend the next hour and a half convincing him to let me talk to you before he tells Dave what he saw. Only I can't talk to you because you totally avoid me and everyone else, and I end up having to stake out your locker. Gee, I don't know, Lauren. Do you think I should be mad?"

I bite my lip and fidget with my hands, my bag sliding off my shoulder. I shrug, trying to get it to sit right, but it just slides right back off. I try again, and Katie reaches out and plucks it off my shoulder, puts it on the floor.

"I asked you," she says quietly. "I asked you—God, I don't know how many times—if something was going on. If there was anything you wanted to talk about. And you never said anything."

"I wanted to."

"Liar." She practically spits the word at me. "You weren't ever going to tell me, were you?"

"I just—I knew you'd be angry and I didn't . . . I didn't know what to say. I mean, Marcus and Dave are good friends, and I know how much you like Dave and how great you think we are together, and like you always say, Dave's perfect. And he is, he really is, but I—I know you don't understand why I like Evan or why I'd want him when Dave is so perfect but—"

"Wait. You thought I'd be mad at you because of Dave?"

I nod. "I—" I look at her. Her mouth is trembling, and, oh God, she's going to cry and I've done this. "I'm sorry," I tell her. "I know I'm a shitty friend. The shittiest. The worst. I just—Katie, I didn't want you to be mad at me. I know I've screwed things up and that I should have said something, but I was afraid and I—"

"You didn't think I'd understand. You thought . . . you thought I'd tell you to stay with Dave."

"Well—"

"God, Lauren. I know you think I'm stupid or something. But I'm not. I know I'm not the kind of friend you want, but I would never . . . You thought I wouldn't listen to you?"

"Katie, no. I don't think you're stupid, I swear. And you're totally the kind of friend I want. It's just—"

She shakes her head. "You really did think that I wouldn't listen. We're supposed to be friends, Lauren. Best friends. And you didn't tell me any of this because you didn't—you didn't think you could. You thought I'd tell you that—what?"

"I don't know," I mumble, and look at my shoes. "I thought you'd tell me all the stuff you did when Dave first asked me out. You said we'd be perfect together and talked about how great he was, how everyone wanted him, about how I was lucky—"

"That's because you said you were lucky! And I told you how great he is and all that other stuff because—" She starts crying for real, and wipes at her eyes angrily. "You just seemed so nervous. All you kept talking about was how he was so nice, how everyone wanted to go out with him. I just wanted you to realize it was going to be okay. So I agreed with you and said you'd be perfect together because I knew he'd totally fall for you."

"You did?"

"Yes. And you thought—that's why you've been hanging out with Gail, right? Because you can talk to her."

"Katie—"

She shakes her head and turns away, fumbles for a paper towel and blows her nose. "Ow," she says after.

"You know," I say hesitantly, "you probably have tissues in your purse. You've got everything in there."

"I know," she says. "But I can never find anything." Her eyes start to well up again, and I never thought . . . I always thought Katie saw me as—well, how I see myself. But she didn't. She doesn't. I walk over to her, my own eyes stinging, and hug her. I think that maybe she'll push me away—and that maybe she should—but she doesn't.

"I'm sorry," I tell her. "I'm so sorry. I should have told you."

"You really thought I'd be mad?"

"Yeah."

She pulls away, sniffles. "I wouldn't have been. I thought you were happy with Dave. You always seemed happy. And then, when all this started, and you were blowing me off I thought—I thought maybe you just didn't want to hang out with me anymore and that I was going to lose another best friend because I'm boring or mean or—"

"Katie, no. It's just—I was scared. And Gail, yeah, she's my friend, and we've started talking and hanging out. But it's not because I don't like you. It's just that—"

"You're finally ready to start letting people in."

I stare at her, startled.

"I told you I'm not stupid," she says, and smiles. "Until recently you've always been . . . I don't know. Kind of closed off. Like, you've never told me anything about your family. I mean, I've met your dad, but I don't know anything about your mom other than that she's not around. But now you're more—I don't know. More here. More like who you are."

She's right. God, is she right. "You may not be stupid," I say, "but I am. I am so stupid, and I'm sorry. I should have told you everything." And then I do. I tell her everything. I tell her about Mom, about how she left and what happened after. I tell her about Dave, about how things really are between us. I tell her about Evan, about how we first met, about how we met again. About where we are now.

"Wow," she says when I'm done. "That's—you—" A snore from one of the pot smokers interrupts her, and we both giggle, the tension between us totally broken.

"You should see your face when you talk about Evan," she says. "You really like him, don't you?"

The bell rings. We both ignore it, and I nod, blushing.

Katie smiles. "You know, I think this is the first time I've ever seen you really happy, Lauren." She hugs me. "I'm glad. I want you to be happy."

"I want you to be happy too," I tell her. "And if you ever want to talk about Marcus or your brothers or anything—"

"I know," she says. "Now come on, or we're totally going to miss second period too."

As we're walking down the hall, we pass Gail. Normally I would worry about what to do, would worry about what Katie would say if she saw me talking to Gail. But now I realize Katie wasn't what was worrying me. I was worrying myself. I was afraid to be me.

I wave at Gail and stop to say hi. Katie stops too, and we all talk for a second. Things aren't perfect—I don't think Katie and Gail will ever have anything in common—but that's okay. I can be friends with both of them. I don't have to hide things anymore. I can be myself.

And now I know what I have to do.

I go to my classes. I pretend I'm listening to whatever it is I'm being told. I wait for lunch to start, and when it does, I find Dave.

"Hey," I say, and put my hand on his arm. "Let's go for a walk."

I don't take him to the benches. I start to, but I can't. Dave deserves more than that from me. So we just walk outside, cross the lawn like we're heading toward the parking lot.

"Are we going somewhere?" he asks, and I shake my head.

"No," I say. "We aren't. That's what I want to talk to you about."

"What?" he says, and stops walking. He is looking at me, his beautiful eyes full of confusion and something else, something almost hidden. But I see it and I know what it is. He knows exactly what I'm saying, and, more than that, I think he needs me to say it. That maybe he wants me to.

"Here's the thing," I say. "We—we don't belong together. What you want isn't what I want. I don't want to go to college around here. I don't want to come home every weekend. I don't want—I don't want things to stay the way they are forever."

"Lauren," he says, "all that's in the future. It's not set in stone. Things can change, I know that. But what won't, and what really matters, is that I love you."

"No, you don't. You want to because you think you should, but you don't. There's no way you could. You don't even really know me."

"Don't know you? Of course I do. And I do love—"

I shake my head, hating the hurt look on his face but knowing I have to do this, that if I don't I'll only end up hurting him more. "What do you love about me?"

"Everything. The way you listen, how you understand the choices I've made. The fact that we never fight, that we always feel the same way about things."

"Exactly," I say softly. "We never fight. We always agree."

"And that's a bad thing?" he says, his voice rising slightly. "The fact that we understand each other, that together we're—"

"Perfect, right?" I say. He nods. "I'm not perfect, Dave. Not even close. Nobody is. If we were really in love with each other things wouldn't be perfect. They couldn't be because nothing real is perfect."

"So I don't know my own feelings?"

"Dave—"

"No, it's fine. I get it. Now that you and that guy—Evan—are together, it totally makes sense. Of course I don't love you, so you've got to break up with me, right?"

I suck in a breath, startled. "You know?"

"Yeah. The day you saw Marcus in the parking lot? I was there too, getting ready to leave. So don't make this about me because it's not. It's about you feeling guilty and trying to make yourself feel better."

"I—I should have told you about Evan before. I know that and I wish I'd been brave enough to. But I think—I think that you and me were always about you wanting to have what your parents do, and me not wanting to be like mine. And you deserve more than that. You deserve someone who truly wants all the things you do. You deserve more than pretending and I . . . I think you know that. I mean, you knew about Evan and you didn't say anything, Dave. You deserve to be with someone you really care about. Someone who, if you saw them with another guy, would make you upset enough to say something."

He's silent for a long moment, and then he says, quietly, "Can I ask you something?"

I tense, but I owe him this. I owe him more than this. "Sure."

"Was I—was I a bad boyfriend?"

I look over at him, surprised. "Never," I say, and watch him fold his hands together tightly.

"Then why—" He breaks off, blows out a breath. "Never mind."

"Dave . . ." Now it's my turn to stare at the ground. He'll be the perfect guy for someone, someday, but he was never perfect for me, and I lied to him, to myself, for no other reason than that I was scared.

"I get it," he says. "What you said, I mean. I don't want to, but I do. But I—I don't want to talk to you anymore right now. I don't even really want to look at you."

"I'm so sorry," I tell him, and I am. He nods once and turns away from me, staring out at the parking lot. I look at his back for a moment, wishing there was something more I could say and knowing that there isn't, and then I walk away.

twenty-four

I walk back into school, head toward Evan's locker. He isn't there but I wait, and when the bell finally rings and people pour into the hallway, I see him. He's walking along with his hair flopping into his eyes like always. It makes me smile. He makes me smile. He sees me and his eyes widen a little.

"So this is a surprise," he says when he reaches me, one of those chewed-off smiles hesitant on his face.

"I just talked to Dave."

"Yeah?"

"Yeah," I say, dying to touch him but not wanting word of it to get back to Dave and hurt him more than I already have. Besides, I know I have time now, that Evan and I will have more moments like this. I know that just like I know that by the end of the day the fact that Dave and I are over will be everywhere and that tomorrow I'll be talked about, judged and found wanting, dismissed back to being a total nobody again.

I can't say I mind.

"So what do you say we get out of here?" he says.

I shouldn't be skipping more classes. I could maybe talk my way out of the two I've missed, but more than that . . . I look at him and he is smiling for real now, broad and beautiful and directed just at me.

"Absolutely," I say, and even if I'm in detention for a year it'll be worth it.

As we walk down the hall I see people staring, and I can almost hear Dave's name on their lips.

I don't care.

Evan and I end up going to the diner where Gail and I met for breakfast. We sit next to each other in a booth, eat fries, and watch people shuffle in and out.

"So you broke up with him, huh?" he says, and I look at him, give in to what I've always wanted to do and reach over, push my fingers through his hair, watching the dark strands as they slide through my fingers. His eyes are serious, intent.

I nod and move my hand down, sliding it along the curve of his cheek to his jaw. I have never wanted to touch anyone like I've wanted to touch him. And now I can do it openly, without worrying who will see. "Yeah," I say softly. "It's official now. You're stuck with me."

"I think I can handle that," he says, and steals some of my fries, leaning over to kiss me when I laugh and steal some of his in return.

We drive to his apartment after we leave the diner. Joe is asleep when we get there, curled up on the sofa, kneading the cushions with her paws. I can see stuffing poking through. "You're gonna have to flip them over soon, " I tell him.

He laughs and says, "You should see the other side," as he heads into the kitchen. I follow him, and in between kisses he tells me he has only a few afternoons left to volunteer at the hospital and makes himself a sandwich to take there today. I look at it when he's finished and trying to find plastic wrap.

"That is one sad-looking sandwich."

"What? It's a masterpiece."

"It's leaking—what is this, pickle juice?—everywhere."

"Hey, I'll have you know making sandwiches is a complicated science. An art, even. You have to get the ratio of stuff to bread just right."

"Stuff to bread?" I say, rolling my eyes. "Oh yeah, I can see you're a master of sandwich making. Pass me the mayo, will you?"

"What are you doing?"

"Making you a real sandwich," I say. "Oh my God, you didn't even drain this tuna before you put it on the bread? You really do need help."

"Maybe I like soggy sandwiches."

"Uh huh. I suppose that's 'thank you' in Evanspeak?"

"No," he says, and comes up behind me, presses a kiss to my neck. "This is. Thank you."

When I'm done making him a real sandwich I scrape the tuna off the other one into Joe's bowl and then laugh as she comes racing into the kitchen.

"Wow, " Evan says, wrapping his arms around me as we watch Joe demolish the tuna and then saunter off down the hall. "Great looking *and* able to feed me and the cat in under five minutes? You truly are a girl of many talents."

"That's right," I tell him. "But don't get any ideas about me doing your laundry." He laughs and I lean back into him for a moment. "So I guess you should drive me back to school so you can get to the hospital."

"I don't have to leave yet," he says, turning me toward him with a smile on his face. We kiss and after a moment he pulls away, cups my face in his hands.

"Stay," he tells me softly, his eyes dark and intent.

"But you have to go—"

"Forget the hospital," he tells me. "I'm going to call Mom and tell her I won't be in to 'volunteer' today."

"Won't she be mad?"

"Yeah, but pretty soon she'll find out about the classes I've missed and that'll distract her."

I sigh. "We're both going to be in detention forever. Except I'll be there longer because I missed first period today too."

"Well, that settles it. I'm definitely not going to the hospital this afternoon, and you and I have to go on a date tonight."

"A date?"

"Yep. Movie, dinner, whatever. I'll think of something."

I laugh and he kisses me, and we head toward his room, sink into his sheets, into each other. When he takes me back to school a few hours later and I drive home, I feel like I'm floating, the memory of his body still warm against me.

Then I walk inside and the feeling vanishes.

Dad is back. He's back and seems upset, is just sitting at the kitchen table turning an empty glass around and around in his hands.

"Hi," I say cautiously. "When did you get in?"

"Late last night. Actually, it was closer to morning. I was home long enough to realize I had an early meeting I couldn't get out of, make some coffee, and oh yes, notice you weren't home. In fact, I was in the car on my way to my meeting, and on my cell on hold with the police, because I was trying to report you missing, when I saw you pull onto our street. Where were you last night?"

"Uh." Oh damn. "Well, I was—I was with Evan."

"Sit down, Lauren. We need to talk." His voice is serious and I think maybe even angry. I don't know. I've never heard him sound like this.

"If this is about Evan, Dad, I really don't want to talk to you about—"

"No," he says. "It's about you and me. And Mom."

"Mom?" My voice comes out high, startled. I can't remember the last time he said her name. I stare at him, and he blinks, looks away, and then looks back at me.

"I don't want to do this," he says. "I'd rather ask about the phone call I got from your school this afternoon telling me you've missed some classes and are going to have quite a bit of detention. I'd rather ask if you're being safe with Evan, if you've thought things through. But there are other things we need to talk about. Things we haven't ever talked about. I'm—this is difficult for me, Lauren. But I've made things difficult for you too, and that's not fair." He motions for me to sit down, and I do. My hands are shaking.

"I've never really told you about her," he says. "I could never bring myself to. I think I always thought, hoped, that maybe she would—"

"Me too," I say, my voice cracking on the words. "But she's not ever coming back, is she?"

He shakes his head. "Your mother and I . . . there were so many things I loved about her, but most of all, I loved how brave she was. I didn't see that it was how she thought she had to be. I never realized that she could be scared. I didn't really know her, in part because I don't think she knew how to let me in, but also because I was afraid. I wanted to be perfect for her because I thought she was perfect. I was afraid to push her to let me closer, afraid that if I did, she'd leave."

"And then she did anyway."

"I don't think she wanted to. Lauren, God, right now, the look in your eyes. She used to look at me like that whenever I said something she didn't believe. But honey, I swear, I don't think she wanted to. I think at first she saw you and me as freedom, a chance for her to escape who she felt she was supposed to be. But then she became my wife and your mother, and she never—I think she felt she never had a chance to be who she really was. I think, in the end, she felt she had no choice."

"So she couldn't be who she was because of you? Because of me? She couldn't—she didn't love me enough to stay?"

"Oh, honey, of course she loved you."

"No," I say fiercely. "I remember, Dad. I remember her always looking out the window, always looking away. Maybe she loved the idea of me, but she didn't—she didn't love me."

He looks at me. I swallow, turn away. I wait for words I know aren't coming.

"It's . . ." he finally says. "Lauren, she and I, we were so young when we got together, and from the start we knew you were on the way. It was overwhelming, but it was amazing too, and I think we thought what we had would be enough, that it would last forever. I didn't realize that being together, being a family—I didn't realize it would take work. I don't think she did either."

"You've never realized that," I say, and it's awful, cruel, but when I say it he doesn't look hurt, just surprised and then a little sad.

"You're right," he says softly. "I never have. I've tried and I've always screwed it up, always been afraid that if it goes on too long it'll end up—"

"Like it did with Mom."

He nods. "I wish—I wish you could have seen her when I first knew her. She was beyond beautiful. She shone. Everyone noticed her, wanted to look like her or be with her. I never really stood out but being with her . . . it made me feel like I was someone. That probably makes no sense to you."

More than you know. "Dad—"

"And I don't want you to think that your mother never loved you or just loved the idea of you. When you were born, Lauren, and she held you in her arms . . . you should have seen her face. She was so happy. I'd never seen her that happy before, not ever. I think it scared her, how much she loved you, but she did love you. And for me, you're—you're the best thing in my life, and I know I don't say it enough, but I lo—"

"Dad—" I mumble, my eyes stinging really hard now. "I know. And you know I—"

"I know," he says gently, and sets the glass down on the table.

"I should—I have to go get ready," I tell him. "I'm going out tonight."

"Evan?"

I nod.

"Lauren—" my father says, and then stops. "I just—I just want to ask you one question."

"All right," I say slowly, bracing myself for . . . well, I don't know. I haven't had much luck in predicting how this conversation would go, that's for sure. But what Dad says next stuns me.

"Does he make you happy?" That's all he asks, and what's more, he looks like he really wants to know what my answer is.

"Yes," I say. "He does."

I can hear Evan's car coming before he pulls into the driveway and smile to myself, go downstairs to wait for him. Dad comes out of his study and stands in the hallway with me.

"You look lovely."

"Thanks."

"You know I meant everything I said earlier."

"I know." I open the door and walk outside, heading toward Evan.

"Hey."

"Hey yourself," he says. "You look amazing."

"You too," I say, and lean over, kiss him. When I turn back around my father is still there, standing in the doorway, watching us with a smile on his face. As we back down the driveway, I wave to him. He waves back, and when we pull out onto the road he's still there, and that's when I know that no matter what, he won't ever leave me behind.

"You ready?" Evan asks, and he's looking at me, and I love his eyes, I love his smile, I love—

"I love you," I say, and as I watch his smile bloom I finally get how great those three little words are. I finally get what they really mean.

LIKE WHAT YOU JUST READ?

TURN THE PAGE FOR A PEEK AT ANOTHER
ELIZABETH SCOTT NOVEL:

PERFECT YOU

one

Vitamins had ruined my life.

Not that there was much left to ruin, but still.

I know blaming vitamins for my horrible life sounds strange. After all, vitamins are supposed to keep people healthy. Also, they're inanimate objects. But thanks to them I was stuck in the Jackson Center Mall watching my father run around in a bee costume.

I sank into the chair by our cash register as Dad walked up to two women. They looked around when he started talking, searching for a way out. They wouldn't find one. In our section of the mall, there wasn't much around, which was how we could afford our booth.

I watched the women smile and step away, an almost dance

I'd seen plenty over the few days I'd worked here. After they left, Dad came over to me, grinning, and said, "Kate, I think I made a sale! Those two women I just talked to said they'd tell their husbands about the reformulated B Buzz! tablets. Isn't that great? Now I think I'll fly—get it?—down to the department store and see if I can give samples to people as they walk out."

I handed over the samples—small plastic bags stamped with the Perfect You logo—and watched him lurch down the hallway, off balance because of his costume. As soon as he was gone, I got out my history homework.

This was not how I'd pictured my sophomore year. Not that the first half had been wonderful so far, but this was definitely an all-time low.

Four hours and one history chapter later, the mall closed. Dad and I boxed up the extra vitamins he'd been so sure we'd sell, and then I waited while he ran the box back to the storage space we rented from the mall.

"Pretty good day, right?" he said when he got back. The antennae he was wearing bobbed up and down as he talked. "Todd and I sold one bottle of B Buzz! in the morning, and I bet those two women come back tomorrow. Don't you think they will?"

I shrugged, because it was much easier than telling Dad I was sure they wouldn't. It was also easier than mentioning that we owed eighty bucks for the rented bee costume, and that was far more than the amount we'd taken in from the one bottle of vitamins it supposedly sold.

When we got home, Mom was sitting at the kitchen table

flipping through the checkbook and frowning. She'd been doing that a lot lately.

"How did it go?" she asked, putting the checkbook down.

I left before she could say anything else, heading back to my room. I took a second to stop in the living room and stand in front of the television though, watching as my brother, Todd, lifted himself up off the sofa long enough to say, "Kate, you freak, move. I'm watching something important."

Last week Todd decided he wanted to be an actor. So far all it meant was that he spent even more time than usual watching television. For a college graduate, he sure was on the fast track to nowhere.

"You can't learn to act watching basketball."

"You can't. I can. Now move."

I started singing and kept it up until he lunged at me.

I have a terrible singing voice, and not in the "I'm saying it's terrible to be modest" kind of way. Last week, when I quit the school choir, the director tried to keep the joy off his face but couldn't quite contain it.

I hadn't cared about that, though. I knew my voice sucked, and quitting was a relief. The only reason I'd stayed as long as I had was because of Anna. All fall I'd suffered through practices, hoping she'd come back. That she'd want to be in choir again. That she'd want to be my friend again.

That maybe she'd at least talk to me again.

In the fall, I thought there was no way life could get any worse.

I was wrong. So very, very wrong.

Almost a month ago, my father got up and went to work at Corpus Software like always, running late because he'd gotten caught up in his latest video game, forgetting about his job in favor of slaying dragons or driving cars or whatever it was that had him obsessed that week.

But then, when he got to work, his desk was broken. Really broken.

It had split right down the middle, and everything breakable—picture frames with photos of all of us, his coffee mug, and the clay thing my brother made during the two weeks he wanted to be a potter—was broken.

The one thing that hadn't broken was a small brown glass jar of vitamins. Perfect You vitamins. Dad had bought them from a secretary who was moving out of town and spent her last day at work selling them. He'd only bought them to be nice.

But, long story short, Dad decided that the whole desk-breaking thing was a sign he needed to change his life, and that the unbroken vitamin bottle meant something.

So he quit his job to sell Perfect You vitamins.

Yes, really.

He cashed in his retirement fund, bought box after box of vitamins, and then rented a tiny freestanding booth in the mall. He even hired someone to work with him, but Gary quit last week, after Dad told him he couldn't pay him. That's when I had to quit choir and start working with Dad after school.

So now I had no best friend, and I had a job at the mall selling vitamins with my father.

Life had definitely gotten much worse.

two

I saw Anna as soon as I got to school the next morning. When Dad dropped me off, she was standing on the sidewalk holding hands with her boyfriend, Sam. She waved in my direction as I walked toward her, and for a second I hoped she was waving at me even though I knew she wasn't. I hated how easy it was for her to act like she'd never known me.

I hated how I still hoped she would notice me.

No one ever asked me why Anna and I weren't friends anymore. I guess everyone automatically understood that when Anna became popular, there was no way she had room in her life for me. Even the Jennifers, three girls I'd tried to be friends with in the fall until I realized they drove me crazy, never asked what happened.

Actually, one person had asked about Anna. Will Miller said, "So what's up with you and Anna?" about a week after school started, but I knew he was just being an ass. Will was like that, one of those guys who was cute and knew it. He'd hooked up with at least half the girls in school, and last year, I swear that every week he made out with a different girl before class. I hadn't liked him since the day I met him.

I tried to avoid him, in fact, but this year he was in my first-period class. It was bad enough I had to start every morning with biology, and Will just made things worse.

For instance, when class was over, we ended up walking into the hall at the same time, and he said, "Hey, what did your frog ever do to you? I saw you hack its legs off."

I sighed. Will always seemed to take some sort of perverse delight in talking to me, but lately he'd been even more annoying about it than usual. "I didn't hack its legs off. My scalpel slipped."

"Wow, promise me you aren't going into medicine."

I glared at him and he grinned, unleashing his dimples. I looked away and saw Anna coming down the hall, walking in the middle of a group of girls we used to make fun of. Two of them waved at Will, and one said, "Any chance we can get you to go shirtless for the next pep rally?"

He shrugged, still grinning, and Anna said, "Think about it, will you?" Her gaze moved over me like I wasn't even there.

I walked away, telling myself I didn't care and wishing I could forget her like she'd forgotten me.

Of course Will caught up to me. "What do you think? Should I do it? I know you've secretly been dying to check me out."

"Right, because if I see your scrawny chest I can die a happy woman." Will actually had a very nice chest. The thing was, he knew that too, because he was always willing to run around shirtless with JHS RULES! painted on him during stupid pep rallies.

"I like that a glimpse of my chest could provide you with the equivalent of a rich and full life."

"The key words in my sentence were 'see your chest' and 'die.' The 'happy' part was me trying to be nice."

"So you say." He unleashed the dimples again, smiling like he knew something, and I felt my face heat up because Will really was cute and I wasn't as immune to him as I wanted to be.

I didn't want him to guess that, though, so I forced myself to look at him. Or at least look at his forehead.

"All right, you caught me. I'm secretly obsessed with you and spend all my free time writing about you in my journal. 'Dear Diary, today Will was an ass for the 467th day in a row. He's so dreamy.'"

He laughed and then leaned in toward me, touching the tip of my nose with his index finger. For some reason, I felt a little breathless. "Are you okay?"

"Aside from you, yes."

Okay, here's the truth. I knew exactly why I felt breathless. I had, let's say, "thoughts" about Will, and not the kind of thoughts I wanted to have, where I was able to forget he existed and also meet an amazing guy who really liked me. No, I had thoughts like me and Will somehow getting trapped in a classroom and Will realizing he wanted me, and I . . . well, let's just say I had a vivid imagination and leave it at that.

The problem was, I had these thoughts a lot. A LOT.

Will put a hand on my arm. It was very warm, and I stared at his fingers resting against my skin, cursing my overactive brain and reminding myself to breathe.

"Seriously, I'm sorry about everything with Anna."

That snapped me out of any "thoughts" I might have been thinking, and I shoved his hand off and walked away. I hated the way I felt around him, the way I wanted him. I hated that he was the only person who'd ever asked me what happened when Anna and I stopped being friends.

I hated that he was the only person who'd acted like her forgetting me meant something.

three

Dad picked me up when school was over, leaving Todd "in charge" at the mall. We went home, so I could change and pack myself some dinner, and he sat on the sofa and played the video game he and Todd had bought and started a few days ago.

I thought it was weird and pathetic that Dad sometimes acted like he was Todd's age or worse, my age, but Mom didn't seem to care and always thought it was funny when he used to call in sick to stay home and finish whatever game he was playing. She said Dad was young at heart, and that he reminded her it was important to have fun.

I would have settled for his kind of fun being less about quitting his job to sell infomercial vitamins, but then I hadn't gotten a say in any of that.

"You want me to pack you something to eat?" I asked him.

He shook his head. "I'll eat when we get home so I can catch up with your mother. She said she'll make pancakes." He grinned at me. "You and me can split a stack. Get it?"

"Funny. And I can't. Homework." I smeared peanut butter on a piece of bread and looked in the fridge for jelly.

"You almost ready to go?"

"Almost." All I could find was orange marmalade. Ick. I finished making my sandwich anyway. With all my homework, plus the fact that I had first lunch block at school, which meant eating before eleven each morning, I needed to eat dinner before I got home from work.

"You look a little stressed," Dad said when we got to the mall. "You want to close up early tonight and go the movies? I want to see the one about the guy who moves into the cursed house."

"I really do have a lot of homework. Besides, Mom's making pancakes, remember?"

"Oh, right, I forgot." He looked disappointed, but then he spotted Todd talking to two girls and darted off in the direction of our booth, waving his arms to try and signal something. I slowed down and hoped no one had seen me come in with him. Sometimes being around Dad was like being with a little kid.

Todd left about ten seconds after I got to the booth, as usual, and when the mall finally closed, the register had twenty dollars less than it had the night before. ("Todd and I forgot to eat breakfast before we came in, so we had to get food and stuff," was Dad's explanation.)

We also hadn't sold a thing.

"Hey, maybe we should take some samples down to Sports Shack and catch people leaving," Dad said. "It's a potential customer base with a built-in interest in staying healthy, plus they always let people shop late."

"Homework," I reminded him again.

"Just for a few minutes? You can even pull the car around while I do it. Okay?"

A chance to drive wasn't something I would pass up, and Dad knew it. I'd gotten my license when I turned sixteen, but Mom refused to let me drive unless she or Dad were in the car until I was seventeen because Todd had driven our car into the garage door two weeks after he'd gotten his license.

And because I'd failed my driving test the first time I took it. But driving over all those cones could have happened to anyone, really.

I went and got the car, then drove over to the parking lot by Sports Shack. Dad was standing by the exit to the parking lot, trying to talk to everyone who came out. I drove around the mall twice, enjoying the feel of being in the car by myself, and when I got back, Dad was talking to an older guy in a Sports Shack uniform, holding his hands out like he did whenever he was sorry about something, and all the employees were standing by the huge floor-to-ceiling windows, watching.

Great. As if the bee costume wasn't enough of an embarrassment. I drove to an unlit portion of the parking lot and waited, hoping no one could see the car. Or me.

"Wow, was that guy uptight," Dad said when he finally got to the car. "I explained that I worked in the mall too, but he didn't care.

Hey, how come you parked way out here? And how come you're sitting all hunched over? Are you sick?"

"Just tired," I said, and was careful to keep my head down as we drove away.

The house smelled like pancakes when we got home, and Mom was on the phone with Grandma. I could tell because she kept rubbing her fingers down the space between her eyebrows like she had a headache.

"No, things are fine," she said, and waved at me, then blew Dad a kiss. "Look, can I call you tomorrow? Great. No, really, please forget what I said before. We'll get by."

She hung up and blew out a frustrated breath. "I think I might have burned some of the pancakes. Sorry." She looked at Dad. "You know how my mother is."

Dad went over and gave her a big hug, lifting her up off the ground. She laughed, and on that almost happy note, I left before she could ask him how sales were. Or before she could really start talking about Grandma.

ABOUT THE AUTHOR

Elizabeth Scott grew up in a town so small it didn't even have a post office, though it did boast an impressive cattle population. She's sold hardware, pantyhose, and had a memorable three-day stint in the dot-com industry, where she learned that she really didn't want a career burning CDs. She lives just outside Washington, DC, with her husband; firmly believes you can never own too many books; and would love it if you visited her website, located at www.elizabethwrites.com.

Looking for something quirky and fun?

Kristen Tracy

Praise for *Lost It*:

★ "Readers will fall in love with this offbeat story."
—*Publishers Weekly*, starred review

"Full of hilarious dialogue. . . ." —*VOYA*

From Simon Pulse | Published by Simon & Schuster